Charles Clarke

Lord Falconberg's Heir

Vol. I

Charles Clarke

Lord Falconberg's Heir
Vol. I

ISBN/EAN: 9783337054922

Printed in Europe, USA, Canada, Australia, Japan

Cover: Foto ©Andreas Hilbeck / pixelio.de

More available books at **www.hansebooks.com**

LORD FALCONBERG'S HEIR.

A Novel.

BY

CHARLES CLARKE,

AUTHOR OF "CHARLIE THORNHILL," "WHICH IS THE WINNER,"
"THE BEAUCLERES," ETC., ETC.

IN TWO VOLUMES.

VOL. I.

LONDON:

CHAPMAN AND HALL, 193, PICCADILLY.

1868.

CONTENTS OF VOL. I.

CONTENTS.

LORD FALCONBERG'S HEIR.

CHAPTER I.

OXFORD AS IT WAS.

' QUIETA non movere.' What a picture! what classic dignity! what philosophic indifference to other people! how wonderfully suggestive of the unprincipled minister of an apathetic sovereign! Let well alone; well, if it be well, certainly! but how if it be bad? be careful not to make it worse. So are we freed from the horns of a dilemma: when the dilemma is progression, which stultifies itself.

Any man who considers the conditions of our constitution, with care and impartiality, will admit that it came to perfection about the time of Edward III. It was then well known to be the admiration of all Christendom. From that time it wanted nothing, and should have been a model to future states and generations. Occasionally a gentle tinkering was demanded for the vessel of the state, more by the know-nothings and the busy-bodies who looked on from the shore, and who claimed to be proprietors, and wiser than other people, than from those who directed the helm, and superintended the rigging, and who must have been the best judges of how far the leak was to be repaired. What is the object of change and renovation so long as battles are won and salaries are paid, and there are ragouts and pure claret for the ten thousand, and a sufficiency of something or other for the million? What could a navvy do with a *meringue*, or a hackney-coachman with a sweetbread stewed in champagne? Little more than with a vote: exchange it for something useful.

How wonderfully the world (of course we mean England and the English) moves on, whoever may be at the helm: Henry II. or the Pope; the King or the Barons; York or Lancaster; a Charles or a Cromwell; a Protestant or a —— (no! we must have an orthodox minister at the head of affairs, for we have always sacrificed even our loyalty to our religion); a Stuart or a Hanoverian; a Pitt, a Fox, a Grey, a Russell, a Peel, a Palmerston, or a Stanley. We have called out loudly once or twice since the Middle Ages, and the governing powers have obliged us, or we should have obliged them. But the action is contemptible enough; and if we are to have many more of these changes, I for one shall begin to think that England and the English are not so infallible as they have always pretended to be.

Now nothing of this sort would come amiss : neither Household Suffrage, nor Vote by Ballot, nor University Extension, nor Inquiry into International Law, if we were willing to admit that we were capable of improvement. But if we are already at the top of the tree, and if we are only bent upon benefiting our neighbours without the acquisition of any advantages from them, why should we give ourselves this trouble and fatigue ? Why paint the lily, or perfume the rose ? Ah ! my fellow-countrymen, there's an element of mock-modesty, a vague suspicion at the bottom of you, which you are willing to satisfy ; or a grand self-sufficiency even in your changes, that whatever your fate, you must be English still. There has been a fine new patch or two put into the old garment, where it has been a little rubbed by long use, or where rough hands have soiled and damaged it ; and now we are strengthening the patch and extending its borders. Some think we are treading on delicate ground and may make the rent worse; but we are a sober, steady set of botchers, and the stitches will do for a long time to come. It's easier to mend the Constitution than to make a new one.

With such sentiments as these my soul had not been so sorrowful over the late changes as it might have been, but for one circumstance. The enemy has attacked our stronghold of happy prejudice, entirely upon the strength of former successes. Oxford, if not fallen, has been gradually sinking, and brazen tongues talk of terrible things. Our sister-universities, if not for all men, were meant for all time. London, Liverpool, Manchester, Suburban villages, Rotten boroughs, Ecclesiastical establishments—I write it with a steel pen softened by tears—all carry with them the elements of change. Their increase, their population, their wealth will increase, and the result is obvious even when John Bright shall be no more. But the very stones of Oxford and Cambridge cry out against it. Those caps and gowns, those princely stomachs, those high tables, bottles, common rooms, and hebdomadal boards, were never intended to crumble away with the old walls and towers, which must go unless Dr Cumming's millennium should save them. Rich mul-

lions, tracery, mediæval transepts, oak and stone,
carry with them the elements of decay; the cater-
pillar and the palmer-worm, and damp and dust,
and the host of destructives, only wait their time
to effect an entrance.   But what matter?   A
Don's a Don for a' that.

So is an undergraduate, with a difference; and
ungraduates, to say truth, are not altogether what
they were.

It was a lovely morning in the winter of 1841,
soft, mild, and genial, when a rather sickly sun
poured as much of its beams as could find its
way through the trees of the garden and over the
wall into the quadrangle of T—— College, Oxford.   It was still early morning, and there was
peace and quiet among the old walls.   The flag-
stones were damp with the mists of the past night,
and but few footsteps had as yet disturbed their
repose.   At this moment, however, from the various little doors which opened upon the pavement
came hurriedly down the creaking old staircases
some thirty or forty young men, in academicals.
By far the greater number were dressed in the
scanty black stuff gown (if it may be so far digni-
fied) and the trencher cap of the commoner of the
university.   Half-a-dozen scholars of the College
wore surplices, and one remarkably handsome

young man made his way to the chapel-door in
the full black silk robes and golden-tasselled cap
of a nobleman. Mr Trenchard, the Dean, slipped
noiselessly in, touching his cap in return to the
morning salutation of the men; and in another
five minutes the porter had closed the doors of
the chapel, and had excluded the idle and un-
punctual.

In another part of the same college, while this
scene was enacting, a young man was lying at
full length on a small iron bedstead. He seemed
to have just awoke from a heavy sleep, and his
scout was pouring cold water into a primitive-
looking tub, now so much the fashion in Paris,
and the substitute for our modern bath. Certain
indications of the previous evening's amusement
were present to casual observation. Two packs
of cards were on the drawers, a dice-box and one
die lay beside them; and mixed up in confusion
with a watch and chain, two or three rings, a
bunch of keys, and a cigar case, were two or three
Bank of England notes crumpled up carelessly,
six or eight sovereigns, and a heap of silver, the
greatest part of which consisted of half-crowns.
Lying on the floor was a pair of trowsers, of some
dark colour, attached by straps to Wellington
boots, denoting the impatience with which the

wearer had drawn them off the preceding evening—
to speak more correctly, at an early hour of the
present day. In one part of the room, over the
back of a chair, lay a black dress-coat and waistcoat—the signs of a demi-toilette—and in another
a shirt still decorated with three convolvulus
leaves of gold and amethyst, attached to each
other by small chains. Such was the fashion of
the day. The whole room was suggestive of anything but monastic asceticism.

'What's the time, Weller?'

'The gentlemen's just gone into chapel, sir.
The bell rung down as I come in, sir.' And
Weller began collecting his master's waifs and
strays, which at first seemed rather a complicated
business. 'Do you hunt this morning, sir?'

'No, but Mr Trevelyan and Mr Beauchamp
are coming here to breakfast, so you must send
for their commons.'

'Yes, sir.' Here Mr Falcon's scout gave the
cold water a turn in the tub, and pitched in the
sponge. 'What time would you like breakfast,
sir?'

'In half-an-hour,' said Mr Falcon, jumping
out of bed, as Mr Weller disappeared; 'and hold
hard,' added he, 'get some kidneys and a spread-
eagle well devilled from Jubber's directly.'

'Yes, sir. I'd better borrow Mr Day's break-fast-service, hadn't I ? '

'No; use your own.'

'Please, sir, we've only got one saucer left. Mr Hickson broke 'em all, shooting with his air-cane yesterday morning.

'Shooting with his air-cane!' said the under-graduate with some surprise, and not quite under-standing the explanation.

'Yes, sir, he was shooting at a picture of his aunt in his own room, and forgot that your scout's room was next to it.'

'Then go and get his crockery.'

'He's broken it all hisself, sir, long ago.' Saying which Weller shut the bed-room door and departed on his errand.

The bed-room door opened upon the sitting-room. It was comfortably furnished, lofty, and sufficiently large for all purposes of use and some of luxury. The curtains were of green stuff with a gold fringe or border, the bookcase of polished oak was handsomely furnished with books, which showed some signs of usage, the carpet was of a warm texture and appropriate colour, the table in the middle of the room was yet laden with cigar ashes and ends, empty and half-empty tumblers, a spirit case, two decanters, and a cigar box, containing some thirty or forty regalias. There were two most luxurious arm-chairs and a couch on either side of the fireplace, which had a cheerful fire already smouldering into a white ash, as the fashion of Oxford coals is and used to be.

The scout had done well to light the fire first—for it continued to throw out a cheerful warmth—and to boil a kettle, while he spread a clean white table-cloth upon the half-rubbed table, and garnished it with cold ham and fowl and the crockery which belonged to Mr Day : Mr Day, who was just now reading out his essay after chapel at the request of Mr President Wig-ram and his fellow Dons.

In half-an-hour from the time he got out of bed George Falcon was sitting in one of his easy-chairs waiting the arrival of Trevelyan and Tom Beauchamp. He was not kept long in suspense. First came a kick on the panels of the door, then the handle turned, and the two guests walked in. They were both remarkable in their way.

Trevelyan was a tall, thin, fair man, scarcely more than boy. He was quiet in manner, but with a prematurely *roué* look about him, which told of hard life before its time, and his pride in it.

Tom Beauchamp was shorter, squarer, with an older and harder look about him. He had a straight line of dark whiskers down his cheek; and a most unaffected joyous smile lighted up his face, as he burst noisily into his friend's room. They both wore their caps and gowns, as they had just come out of chapel.

'I say, Falcon, your name was called for your Essay, to read out.' 'And what did they say?' inquired Falcon carelessly.

'Long looked disgusted, so did the President; and the Dean made a note of it.' Then Mr Weller walked in with the rest of the breakfast; split-fowl and truffles, with devilled kidneys.

'Please, sir, the Dean wishes to speak to you,' said he, as he proceeded to dispense Mr Jubber's dainties.

'Very civil of the Dean: I shall be at home till luncheon.' Here the scout laughed modestly, and added,

'He desired me to say that he wished to see you at his room, sir, at ten o'clock.'

'Then you go and tell him I'm out.' And Mr Falcon poured out the tea.

'These things are deuced uncomfortable,' said Tom Beauchamp at this conjuncture, hitching away at a pair of flannel cricketing trowsers, which he wore under a rough pea-jacket of the period.

'Then take them off,' said Falcon, laughing, but scarcely expecting that he would do so.

'I was just going to,' replied Tom, at the same time throwing open his upper garments, and unbuttoning his braces, with wonderful coolness, while his companions looked on with surprise. 'I was just going to, and all I hope is that they haven't taken the polish off my boots. Oh no, it's all right,' added he, as stepping out of his flannels, he presented himself in a very neat but workmanlike pair of leathers and tops, and letting fall his cap and gown and overcoat, displayed a swallow-tailed pink, and a blue plush waistcoat, of the fashion of the day.

'That's not a bad idea: where are you going, Tom?'

'To the Heythrop. Jim Hills is as good as a run, going from cover to cover. Weller, get my hat, please, out of my rooms; it's on the small table by the window: and now let's eat.' After a pause, he said, 'who do you think I saw at Woodstock yesterday, Falcon?'

'Haven't the least idea, unless you mean Peggy Jansen.'

'Well, I don't—I mean your cousin Harold.'

'Impossible.'

'Why impossible? He was here last week: for he lost a hundred pounds in Christ Church.' Here Tom Beauchamp helped himself to tobacco.

'I didn't know he'd a hundred pence to lose,' said George.

'I thought he was the monied man of the family.'

'I am at present; I won seventeen pounds here last night,' said Falcon, laughing. 'What took you to bed so early?'

'Well, I don't play,' replied Beauchamp. 'You fellows can afford it, I suppose. I can't. I find about two days' hunting a-week as much as I can manage: and I'm obliged to hire every now and then to do that.' Trevelyan said nothing: gambling was a sore subject to him. And just then Tom Beauchamp's scout told him that his hack was outside the gates; so he prepared to go.

'Do you feel sure that you saw Harold Falcon yesterday at Woodstock?'

'Sure: he was not on the main road, but riding down the lane which runs at right angles to the road, about a mile and a half from the town. He was on a chestnut with three white legs?'

'Of course: then he had been out with

Drake, and was going back to Waterpark: he's always there now,' replied his cousin.

'On the contrary. He wore a great coat, and rode in dark-coloured trowsers. He seemed to be coming from the old farm-house in the fields. I've never been introduced to him, but I knew him just as well as I know you.' George Falcon's face grew a shade or two paler, while Tom Beauchamp stated his impressions of Harold Falcon's presence near Woodstock; but he was recovering himself rapidly when Tom added in a careless good-humoured way, 'I do believe that's the very house that Peggy Jansen is said to live in, with some old curmudgeon of a father. But Trevelyan will tell you all about that, Falcon; it's more in his line than mine, and I shall be late at cover.' Saying which, putting his hat firmly on his head, and passing the string through the armhole of his waistcoat on to one of the buttons, this steady-going lover of the chase left the room.

CHAPTER II.

A SELFISH LOVE.

No sooner had the echoes of Tom Beauchamp's steps died away than the two young men,
who remained behind lounging and smoking,
looked up at one another with a serious air.
Something in the late communication had disturbed George Falcon and Trevelyan, to judge of
their countenances.

'Do you believe it was your cousin Harold
that he saw?'

'I do. He could hardly have been mistaken;
and yet I cannot understand how or why he was
there. I know he's at Waterpark, which is only 20
miles off; but he has a very heavy match coming
off (for the race is reduced to a match), and I
hardly expected to hear of him in this county.'

'What could he be doing? He doesn't train
anywhere about there?'

'Not he: he hasn't a horse of any kind,
excepting a couple of hunters which he hired at

Waterpark by the month. The white-legged chestnut is one of them.'

'Has he ever seen the girl?' said Trevelyan again, with more appearance of concern than he had yet shown.

'Not that I know of. He's never mentioned her.'

'Would he have done so, had he known her?'

'Undoubtedly; he's the greatest fool alive about money and women; and a perfect sieve as regards both. He has spent every shilling he ever had; and would tell you every secret he ever knew, whether it concerned himself or his friend.'

'You speak feelingly, George, of your cousin's weaknesses: has he ever robbed you of the one or the other?'

'He never had a chance; and never shall,' added George Falcon after a pause, setting his teeth, and evidently by his fixed eyes looking into some speculation beyond the present moment. 'He never shall have the chance. Harold Falcon is a second brother's son. He has squandered, or given away (which is the same thing), all he ever had, and that was not much; and as to a woman, I don't suppose he ever cared for anything but a racehorse in his life, though they say there's a woman or two cares for him.'

'Illo ter est felix—happy dog.   Who's the woman ? '

'His cousin, Lady Helen, Lord Falconberg's daughter, I'm told.   When he's quite done, they can retire upon whatever the old lord will give them, and twenty thousand pounds of her own.'

'Does he know of his luck ? ' said Trevelyan, yawning.

'Not he.   Never goes near them, excepting to shoot the covers.   He scarcely knows Helen by sight.   Besides, she is but a baby after all.'

'What's he mean to do, if he's so awfully hard-up as you say ? '

'Oh, just now he's going to break the ring. I believe he's made a wonderful book on the Waterpark steeplechase, by which he stands to win four thousand to nothing.   So he says, at least.   He did back the Rover at a long price, I believe, and he's been first favourite for some time at a very short one.   He's had a good hedge, and the bet was made with Cranstone.   What are you going to do, Trevelyan ? '

'I'm going to Charley Simonds's, and then to lecture.'

'Will you go to Woodstock with me ? ' inquired Falcon, somewhat eagerly.   'The pictures at Blenheim not being the attraction.'

'Yes; I don't mind if I do. You want some-body to look after you when you're there.' Falcon blushed—he could still blush—and then laughed uneasily. 'What time will you go?'

'After luncheon—two o'clock. We can dine at Dickenson's when we come back: or the Mitre, if you like it better. We're sure to be late for hall.'

'Then go to Tom Perrin's, and order a buggy to be at the gates at two—get the old grey if you can.'

'All right.' Saying which Trevelyan left the room.

When he was gone George Falcon got up, and stood a few seconds with his back to the fire. Then he took down a book or two from his shelves, but it would not do. He couldn't read. So he began to think again; and his thoughts all went one way, or ended in one precipice—it was a precipice—Peggy Jansen and Woodstock. And his cousin Harold. 'What the d—l had Harold to do at Woodstock, or within miles of old Jansen's house, if indeed it was he?'

In those days, up to a certain point, university life was very like what it is now, and what it always must be; and which neither Gathorne Hardy nor Mr Gladstone will avail to alter.

From ten to twelve, then as now, the hive was in full work. In and out of their little monastic holes, about the quadrangles and about the gardens, came the bees—drones many of them—caps and gowns on their heads, and the signs of knowledge under their arms, anthropophagi (metaphorically there they carried their heads). The time of lecture had arrived : and those who were not engaged in chasing the fox, or driving four-in-hand, were usually to be found in attendance. There were certain men with whom the former of these amusements was always a valid and admitted excuse. Tom Beauchamp was one of these.

' Where were you yesterday, Mr Beauchamp ? ' said the vice-president and tutor. ' I missed you at my lecture.'

' I beg your pardon, sir : I went to Bicester Windmill,' replied Tom, who kept his own horse, and had an acknowledged permission from the Parent-Beauchamp to spend a certain time in the field. The eldest son of a fox-hunting baronet might have done worse.

' You might have asked for leave of absence, sir, at all events.'

' I sent my scout, sir, to ask if you were in, and I found you were gone out, and not likely to return in time,' said the unabashed.

'Another time, write a note, sir. You have not encroached on your usual allowance of days, I hope.'

'I think not, sir.'

'Nor of horseflesh either, I trust. We are anxious to restrict that pernicious habit of hiring as much as possible, Mr Beauchamp. It's the ruin of men: they never know how much they owe, nor the misery of owing anything till it's too late. Good-morning. Will you ask Mr Trevelyan to come to my rooms, if you should happen to see him?'

And after awhile Trevelyan came, the youngest son of a younger son, of good birth, and no expectations beyond hard work in the colonies, or still harder in the Temple, for which he was fitting himself by self-indulgence and dissipation.

'I must ask you to write out yesterday's lecture, Mr Trevelyan; the habit of neglecting it is increasing in the college, and must be noticed.'

'I beg your pardon, sir, I was out hunting; and should have asked you if you had been in college in the morning.'

'Were you riding your own horse, Mr Trevelyan, or a hired one?'

'A hired one, sir.'

'Does Dr Trevelyan approve of your hunting?'

'He allows it when I'm down, sir,' replied Trevelyan triumphantly.

'On hired horses at two guineas a day, with a hack at a shilling a mile, six shillings the man's expenses, and a dinner at an hotel in the evening? Scarcely, I think, sir. Will you spare me five minutes' conversation, Trevelyan,' says his tutor in an altered and kinder tone. 'Sit down, if you have time; if not, come to me in the evening after hall.' And Trevelyan sits down, and his tutor points out to him the evil course he has entered upon—shows him the difference between himself and the Beauchamps—reminds him of the prospects of the one and the other—and excuses the authorities of Alma Mater for being all things to all men. It makes an impression on some for the time, on some for eternity. When the seed and the ground were well selected, in the middle of all our barrenness, it was the sprouting moment of much good fruit.

When Trevelyan left Falcon's rooms, he went to Charles Simond's stables, and engaged a horse for the next Saint's-day. There were more prayers and no lectures on those days, so they were devoted to hunting with impunity. Tom Beauchamp rode sixteen miles to cover in an hour and a quarter. All who were in college imagined themselves busy until twelve o'clock, and then they began to think of luncheon, oyster patties, hot kidneys, Stilton cheese, and bottled stout; and the last dun sneaked out as the first pastry-cook's boy entered.

On the day in question neither the dean, nor the principal, nor any of the tutors sent for Mr Trevelyan to advise him or to impose him. The first had been tried without great success, when he was supposed to be more amenable to impression; the latter had been found to be almost as expensive as the hunting and tandem-driving it was meant to rectify; and put sovereigns by the score into the pocket of Bendell the hatter, who made a handsome thing out of the Bible-clerks, servitors, and middle men. Indeed a poor college would be a useful institution if things go on so now.

Dress is said to have a moral effect upon man. If it be true—and I can scarcely doubt it—that a gentleman in dirty boots, a ragged coat, and badly-made trowsers, feels himself less a gentleman than heretofore, then it is true that a difference of style portrays or creates a difference of character. So great is the alteration in this respect that five-and-twenty years have produced, that it is worth while to note the toilette of an Oxford

man of the period of which we are speaking, lest
in a few years' time no recollection of it shall remain, and the fashion shall have become as obso-
lete as the old stage-coach and the science of
driving it.

Trevelyan was a fair average specimen of the
university mode of thirty years ago; and as he
prepared for his drive to Woodstock it was manifest that he was taking some pains to appear to
the best advantage. Let us look at him as he
emerged from his bed-room in search of his hat
and gloves.

He was tall and a good figure; and without
any pretensions to beauty looked like a gentleman.
Moses and Son, and Nicholls and Co., did not
then exist; or if they did, cheap and ready-made
clothing had not yet reached the Universities.
It would have been as impossible for his valet to
have looked like a gentleman as it would have
been absurd for him to have dressed himself like
his valet. His boots were known as Wellingtons
of the best make, of patent leather, and as much
made for ornament as for use. Indeed, here I
am reminded of the great Mr Last, and an anecdote of those times: 'Boots not wear well? bless
my heart, sir, you have been walking in those
boots:' and so he had, and so did we, and so did

Trevelyan. They were not so well fitted for
that as for his foot, but they were not like the
clodhoppers in which Young England rejoices
now, and against which the stones in the High-
street cry out. His trowsers fitted him as they
could have fitted no one else, and were strapped
closely over his instep by a piece of the cloth
which buttoned under the arch of his well-turned
foot. The trowsers were cut straight, and among
well-dressed men indulged in no *ins* and *outs*
about the leg. Such things had been, but were
not at the time that Trevelyan made his toilette. What shall I say in praise of his coat?
a frock-coat of course. It fitted him too, which
is more than can be said of coats since Members
of Parliament have taken to making them. It
was of a soft flexible cloth, with a roughish nap,
and a velvet collar. It was buttoned closely
from the waist upwards towards the throat, showing to advantage the clean and manly figure of
the wearer; and only sufficiently open to exhibit
a neat tie of black and gold, finished by an elaborate pin—a death's head of gold and enamel, joined
to a cross-bones by a small chain. His neck was
not the vulture-like affair which obtains in modern
days, nor did he scud under bare polls—a fashion
which semi-Byronic affectation has crossed with

continental foppery. It was decently enfolded
in a clean well-starched linen collar (not dog-
collar), which reached the level of the incipient
whisker, and terminated near the point of the
chin on either side. Such was Trevelyan as he
came from his afternoon toilette to drive with his
friend George Falcon: can any modern undergraduate say as much, or declare that he ever
gave the same attention to please other people as
to gratify his own lazy indifference.

As he took up his hat—ah! I had nearly forgotten—you might have looked long through
every room in T—— before you would have seen
a billy-cock, a sombrero, a felt, a coal-heaver, or
a wide-awake. A Lincoln and Bennett, or mine
ancient friends, Locke or André, served our turn.
And the old chimney-pot, the despised of your
young athletes, and the football of your Reform
demonstrations, was worn for everything but to
beat a cover, or pull in a racing-boat. The latter
amusement was not the fashion in those days, but
we flattered ourselves we could ride. As he took
up one of his hats, for there were about half-a-
dozen in different stages of consumption from the
severity of the drag, and some falls with the
Heythrop and Drake, and a generally wet season,

he looked like an English gentleman fulfilling the objects of a university career.

'Are you ready, Falcon?'

'Very nearly; let me get a shawl; we shall be late, and the nights are cold—and—yes—it's all right, the cigars are in my great-coat pocket.' Saying which the two leisurely left the college.

There was nothing remarkable in Woodstock in those days. A quaint little country town, with scarcely a street in it; an old town-hall and a market-place, and a few public-houses and hotels for the coaches, of which inns the principal was the 'Bear.' Mine host was a cheerful good fellow, who brewed excellent egg-flip on a cold day, and knew an Oxford man instinctively. The trade of the town was not great, and the business was only brisk for half-an-hour a day, when the 'Defiance' dined and changed horses, or when thirty or forty undergraduates got on their hacks, leaving their horses, jaded and dirty with the white mud of the Oxfordshire hills, to come on after their gruel. But there was a trade, and its sole representative apparently was one Thomas Brown, and that trade was 'gloves'—men's, women's, and children's gloves—and all other articles of wear in white leather: Woodstock we called it.

At five o'clock in the afternoon in question, there turned into Thomas Brown's shop two young men; there being already no less than four leaning over the counter, and three more discussing the beauty of Polly Brown, outside of the door, preparatory to investing in gloves, braces, or some useless little present of female apparel; for it's difficult to say what there was not to be found ready made in Woodstock leather.

The four men leaning over the counter were breaking a lance with stout Mrs Brown and her daughter Polly; and there was so much of laughter and trying on of gloves and recommendation of goods, that the new comers waited a minute or two unheeded, but not for long. An inner door opened, through the glass of which a view into the front shop was easily obtained, and then came forward and took her seat in a vacant chair in the corner, a person, whom it would be difficult to forget, having once seen. Her face grew a shade paler at first, as she came in, but it was again suffused with a deeper red, and her eyes filled with conscious tears, as she and one of the new customers looked at one another. Trevelyan, for it was he and Falcon, turned away from the two, and lounging with his back to the counter, continued to watch with a satirical smile the

open flirtation with the four men who were unknown to him. Falcon and the girl whispered a
few words to one another, and she then began
to make pretence of searching for some gloves
that would fit him.

While he was trying the gloves listlessly, she
might have been seen to write a line or two upon
a piece of note-paper, and, folding it hastily, to
push it towards the young man. George took it
apparently unperceived; and leaving the gloves
on the counter, with the exception of one pair,
he regarded the girl once more with a look of
great affection, nodded to Mrs Brown, and left the
shop.

'Trevelyan, are you going to do anything for
an hour or two? I can't go yet, old fellow, and
we can't dine now.'

'Not very well, certainly, but I'm going into
the park to speak to one of the keepers about a
dog of mine, which he professed to break for me.
What time shall we start? It's dark at six.'

'I'll be ready at seven; there's a moon; and
we shall be back by eight.' Saying which George
Falcon lounged into the stable, and Trevelyan
went in search of the keeper.

It was just getting dark—so dark as to render
it difficult to distinguish persons unless well

known—as a well-dressed woman turned silently
out of Woodstock towards Banbury. She looked
neither to the right nor left until she reached a
grass lane with a gate half opened at the end, and
leading apparently only towards the fields. Here
she stopped a moment, and raised her veil stealthily, looking back along the road she had come,
and then endeavouring to penetrate the twilight
towards the field.

In the latter direction she thought she distinguished the outline of a man's figure, and turning
abruptly through the gate, she hurried towards
it. She was right; a hundred yards up the lane
her lover—for such he professed to be—was waiting for Peggy Jansen.

He passed his hand through her arm, pressing
it kindly, and walked by her side for a few paces
in silence.

'So you are come, Margaret, at last,' said
George Falcon.

'Always, as I have promised,' replied the girl,
with an accent and manner slightly foreign; 'but
you have waited—I couldn't help it, I was wanted.'

'Oh, not long,' said he, however, with a somewhat injured air; 'but it always appears tedious
when waiting for you,' in the same breath making the amende. The first ebullition was very

natural to him, perhaps the last not less so.

Then he spoke very kindly to her of things concerning himself, and afterwards on ordinary subjects; but to these last she answered never a word. She only clung closer to George as they walked very slowly, stopping underneath an old straggling hedgerow and dilapidated wall, which rose on their left hand, and which enclosed partially some large grazing grounds, once an old park or pleasaunce. Once or twice George thought he detected a sob, but pretended not to have heard it, as indeed it was much suppressed, for he was a man who liked nobody's blue devils but his own; and though he thought he loved, or said to himself that he loved Margaret Jansen, he didn't like her tears.

'Turn back, George, we mustn't go any farther this way,' said the girl.

'And why not this way?' inquired George Falcon.

'That's my home down in the hollow, and if my father should see us—'

'What then, Margaret?'

'He would kill you, perhaps, and me certainly;' and she clung closer to him, as if she partially realized the impression.

'I think not, Peggy. I can take care of myself at all events; and why should he kill me?'

'If he knew all—' and to any one who could have seen the faces through the dusk of early evening, his would have seemed paler, and hers burning with a conscious blush.

'But why need he know all?' But Margaret Jansen hid her face against her lover's shoulder, and sobbed convulsively. Then George Falcon stopt, and spoke soothingly to the poor girl till she was calmer.

'George, George, there is but one way, and you promised. You must marry me, now indeed you must;' and she continued to sob, hiding her lovely face against his shoulder still. But George didn't answer; and as Margaret became redder and redder he only became paler and colder.

At length he said, closely pressed upon the subject: 'Marry! ah, Peggy;' and here he sighed, 'if you only knew the difficulties. Wait, dearest, you must wait. How should we live, and I not through my degree.' Then the girl raised her head, and her clasp grew less tight, and for the first time an impression was left upon Peggy Jansen that she never knew George Fellowes (he had told her that that was his name) until now. Her confidence in his promise had never been shaken until this moment. It might have been

that she had never urged it so strongly, or clung
to its fulfilment with such absolute necessity. Her
blushes were gone, and had given place to the
pallor of fear. She bore his caresses now rather
than met them.

'And when shall I see you again, Margaret?'
said he as he wandered on by the old broken
wall, thinking more of himself and the conse-
quences to him of his wickedness, than of her
and the ruin to her consequent upon her weak-
ness.

'You know where to find me, George, every
day, and all day long. If not, come and look for
me at home. But not now. Be careful, George,
my mother suspects me; and if my father knows
it, I have no other hope but you.' They had wandered on during these last few words farther
than they had yet come, when the girl suddenly
stopt, suppressed a scream which rose to her lips,
and motioned George Falcon to fall behind her.
A low door at the farther end of the wall, with
which he was unacquainted, had opened, and
through the darkness a huge figure, made still
larger by the peculiar conditions of the atmosphere, suddenly crossed the path. 'Hush! My
father,' whispered she; 'back, behind me, adieu,
quick, away as fast as you can. George was no

coward, save as far as his conscience made him
so; but Peggy's terror imparted itself to him,
and he began to retreat, as the enormous figure
in the distance came slowly towards the girl.

If George, as he gained the road in safety, had
honestly put his feelings into words he might
have said, 'Poor girl, that was a disagreeable,
but fortunate interruption, for I should never
have got away.'

'All right, Trevelyan,' said he walking into
the parlour of the 'Bear,' and ringing the bell for
the ostler.

'So it ought to be, for I've been waiting three
quarters of an hour. I felt strongly inclined to
start without you,' replied Trevelyan, good-humouredly.

'Why didn't you then? I should,' said the
other ungraciously.

'I can easily believe it.' And so they drove
back to Oxford.

Nevertheless, George Falcon did love the girl
after his selfish fashion, and was always pining
after her when he was away from her. He wasn't
a favourite with men, and missed Margaret's expressions of affection, hasty and stolen as they
were.

CHAPTER III.

PEGGY JANSEN.

THE going back reminds one of an Irishman's mode of progression in the mud; but disagreeable as it is, it is necessary to do so for the clear intelligence of our story.

As Peggy Jansen has something to do with the interests of the principal persons concerned, the reader will be glad to know who she was, and how she came into the position in which we find her.

Her father, Bernhard Jansen, was a very extraordinary person, and his adventures would almost have furnished matter for a novel of themselves. We may take another opportunity of gratifying any curiosity on the part of our readers. At present he is subordinate to those with whom he is acting.

He was of Dutch extraction, but had become a naturalized German, living in Nuremberg, and supporting himself by an extraordinary talent for wood-carving, at the time he fell in with his wife, the mother of his only child, Margaret. He was a man of gigantic stature, of great strength, of a saturnine humour rather than a really evil disposition, and of much taste and even genius in his calling. He was known to have been a smuggler, and it was thought a pirate; and the peaceable Nurembergers said, whatever they believed, that der Herr Jansen had sold himself to the devil. Perhaps he had : if so, that mysterious purchaser of bad bargains had not given much for him, unless the money had gone somewhere else, for with all the exercise of his craft Herr Bernhard remained but poor.

In the matter of women he was not speculative, and Frau Jansen was the first he had affected. She was an English woman, as remarkable in her way as he in his, and accepted him most unconditionally. She had followed the fortunes of an English family who lived at Stuttgard, and when they returned to England had chosen to remain behind, as the show-woman in one of those toy and curiosity shops so numerous in the old cities of Germany. She was an astute, clever woman, master of herself, which is much, and of other people, which is more, and of her husband, which is most. Still, after a time, with all his talents and hers too, they didn't get on. They lost money: and Bernhard Jansen was not the man to sit calmly by and see his all go without a struggle. He tried the bourse as a last resource, and that failed.

'My dear, the air of Nuremberg is not good for me.'

'Then let us go,' said she without a murmur.

'What, and give up our business here?'

'No, but sell it.' And as they kept their secret, and Bernhard had acquired a reputation, they didn't leave Nuremberg empty-handed. They spoiled the Egyptians before leaving.

'And where shall we go, liebe Frau?'

'Let us try England. I have friends there.' And in a few weeks they landed. He, she, and her little daughter, the Peggy of whom we write.

It so happened that at that time a taste for old carving was being cultivated. The taste was not yet purely ritualistic; but Oxford had commenced a movement, which combined high art with religion. Bernhard had none of the latter, any more than his wife, but he had much of the former. So much that Wardour Street gave him high wages, and he might have done well. For the world, that is, the antiquarian world, liked his humour as well as his work. But he would gamble. He tried everything: the Stock Exchange, the hells of the quadrant, the race-course. Having borrowed then as much as he could, he took to lending—this was his wife's suggestion. They began to grow rich, which men soon do who lend a little money at sixty per cent. But the professional money-lenders didn't like him; and his size made him conspicuous. He began to be known in the courts, and an awkward case or two among subalterns in the army did him no good. It was time to beat a retreat.

Bernhard felt no intense admiration for Frau Jansen, but he loved his little daughter Margaret, who was growing into a beauty. He consulted his friends, and he heard of a tumble-down farmhouse ten miles from Oxford, where he might be out of the way of some importunate creditors, and yet work diligently at his calling. The house was to be had at a nominal rent. It was of no great value; large and commodious, out of repair, every room in it big enough for a workshop. Frau Jansen, too, had an idea; and as it involved ambitious thoughts for her daughter, that neighbourhood did as well as, or better than, another.

Frau Jansen thought that her daughter might marry a gentleman. She was quite good-looking enough for it; and, as the manner of foreigners is, her education had fitted her for it. In the mean time she must help them to live : there must be no drones in the hive. It was not difficult. The trade of Woodstock furnished the means. The girl was quick and handy : she became valuable as a skilful glover; and her beauty made her acceptable to Mrs Brown, as an attraction. Oxford went· raving mad after Woodstock gloves, capes, pelerines, and tippets, bordered with lace; and Peggy Jansen became the reigning toast. But Peggy had been taught to carry her pitcher to the well without breaking it, and for some time she succeeded.

The farm was a dull house; and Bernhard Jansen's mode of life did not tend to enliven it. Sometimes he felt dull himself, and then he called for his daughter as King Cole would have called for his beer.

'Mother, what good does Peggy at our friend the glover's?'

'Mind your own business, Giant.'

'*Sapperment!* it is mine own business. What makes the girl there?' said he, in his own idiom.

'She makes money, and that's something. Every little helps.'

'But I don't want the little helps: I prefer Peggy.' And Herr Jansen was not far wrong, for at eighteen Peggy was a very charming girl.

'Attend to your carving, Giant. I tell you the girl will do well enough. There's scores of them coming to see our Madge every term. It isn't gloves or tippets they want: wait a bit—'

'Wait a bit, indeed. What's that? Don't let me hear that, Mrs Jansen. Would you sell your own flesh and blood for a mess of pottage? *Verdamme mich*, will they marry my daughter?' And Jansen rose, dashing down the tools with which he was working.

'Will they marry your daughter?—and why not, pray? I suppose they may look at her first. A cat may look at a king. There, go on working: don't be alarmed about Margaret while she's with me?' The giant retired growling, like a disturbed and incredulous mastiff as he looks at the butcher's boy, and sees that, if not a thief, he is at least the representative of one.

But time reconciles man to much. It reconciled Bernhard Jansen to his wife's arguments, and to the fact of his daughter doing something for her livelihood. Life is uncertain; and though he had good employment and wages, and could find money for other people, the Old Farm, as it was called, became more dilapidated, Frau Jansen had less money in the old stocking, and the carver did not improve in temper as in times of prosperity.

We come now to an extraordinary page in Jansen's life, and to its explanation. When employed as a professional gambler, and a race-commissioner, he had made a large but mixed acquaintance. A stentor, of some six feet six in height, and of proportionate circumference, can scarcely shout ' Seven to one, bar one,' for many weeks without being noticed and known. Jansen was known, and known favourably. And he was known favourably because, though not a fortunate man nor a rich one, he would wait for his money. And he had many opportunities of practising patience. For either the times were bad (they always are so), or the morals of the rising generation were bad : and when they ought to have paid their losses, they were always desiring to negotiate bills. And by some means or other, quite inexplicable to himself, and therefore to his wife and other people, Bernhard Jansen got into the way of discounting them. He would have made money, but he had none ; or spent it as soon as he could get it : and in the matter of money he only acted as the agent of other people. He was popular with his customers; and the men liked to come to his house to look at his carving and his pictures, his curiosities and his daughter.

'Where's that money going to, Giant? It's wanted here.'

'That's going to a great swell, Dame Jansen, to pay his book.'

'And what do you call a great swell?'

'He has no money and many friends. Their name is good.'

'You mean legion.'

'No, I mean good—good to sound and good to write. They look well upon paper, and my friends like them in the city.' So Bernhard Jansen became and continued a bill-discounter; receiving sixty per cent. for other people, and getting five for himself, with all the credit of the transaction.

And this is how Peggy Jansen found herself at Mrs Brown's, cutting out, or rather sewing, Woodstock leather, and the admiration of the undergraduates, who buzzed round her, like flies round a honey-pot, till they found there was no reciprocity of attachment. Then they turned to the responsive beauties of Jane Brown and her sister, who regarded all undergraduates as made for the conversion of their silver into Browns.

But Peggy's was a position of much temptation : and though perseverance even in such pursuits is not a speciality of university life, which rather deals with the innocence of butterfly persecution than determined siege ; still that immunity from danger which is said to arise from numbers is in these cases wanting : and a spurious imitation, called *passion*, sometimes usurps the place and fulfils the office of a holy love. It must not be supposed that Mrs Jansen had thus knowingly exposed her daughter to such dangers. She was a clever and a cunning woman ; and overreached herself for lack of that worldly experience, which never belongs to women in her class of life. Experimentally she knew nothing of such temptations : had she known them it would only have been to have laughed at them : and to say truth, she scarcely believed in their existence. Those who fell she thought to be radically bad, which she knew. Peggy was not ; and those who failed in attaining an honourable pre-eminence among their equals, she believed to want the foresight and the attractions which Peggy possessed. Mrs Jansen was a schemer ; but not so deliberately wicked as she ought to have been for her punishment.

For it is a melancholy truth that Margaret fell

in love, not with an open-hearted, soft-headed,
inexperienced rattlebrain as she might have done,
and followed her mother's prescription of marrying him out of hand, and calling herself a lady
for life, but with a hard selfish nature, who was
sure to turn his conquest to his own account,
without regard to her. From the beginning he
had schemed as deeply as the mother, and so
safely that it was no hard-fought battle. He
gave her no opportunity of withdrawing her queen
before it was checked and taken. He had given
a wrong name, he had promised all that she could
have asked for, and to the last moment she believed her betrayer. He might have believed too
in his will to fulfil all his promises, for he was in
love as such men are. But circumstances were
much against him. He was not his own master
in the eye of the world, though uncontrolled or
nearly so by positive ties. He could have made
an honest man of himself—the world would have
called it making an honest woman of poor Peggy—
if he had pleased. But there were obstacles and
feelings that required fighting, and that fighting
was not to be done by a soldier who had only
trained himself to run away. 'Because I have
been a blackguard, shall I forsooth be a fool too?
And yet, poor girl, what beauty it is; and if it

could only be hushed up, why shouldn't I be
happy with her? I'm sure I shall never love
any one as I do Peggy. And what are my prospects after all? The colonies! well, why not?
There are too many of us Falcons about in this
country to get a loaf apiece.' With which vague
notions he lit a cigar and began to think, as he
urged Trevelyan to get on faster. Margaret went
home on the arm of her father, whose ominous
silence boded no measured language when he
should think fit to speak.

CHAPTER IV.

OUR HERO, SUCH AS HE IS.

AMONG those whose necessities had brought them in contact with Herr Jansen, was one of whom we shall hear more as the story progresses. He was one of many, but with his idiosyncrasies, which make him an interesting study of a rather uninteresting class. Harold Falcon belonged to the aristocracy, Eton, Oxford, the Guards. There was a time when such antecedents might have impressed the world favourably. They have the elements of cheerfulness, intellect, fashion, heroism. But now we want mystery, gloom, crime, improbability. And if we can only plead that the facts be taken from real life, that the poisoner was our own familiar friend, that the mystery belonged to a real cupboard, and the arsenical mixture to a living chemist, what revision shall be bold enough to take us to task? Who shall say that slow poison is not the universal curse (like Latin verse) of

'67, or that the normal condition of society is not death by fire or suffocation in a well.

But in '41 it was not so. Men and women, that is, ladies and gentlemen, died in their beds, or intended to do so. They did odd things—they spent too much money ; they went first to the Jews and then to the dogs; they formed questionable connections, or married as they should not ; they robbed one another; became unexpectedly rich, unexpectedly poor; they gambled, they raced, but they lived in good houses, and were to be found in the pale of society. The common vices of the great world were neither bigamy, larceny, nor murder; and when noblemen and gentlemen are concerned in such things, depend upon it the cases are exceptional.

It is but fair to the coming generations to declare thus much. We have read of Corporal Trim, Matthew Bramble, Parson Trulliber, and we know that they existed as they are represented to have done. Fielding and Smollett painted society as they knew it : sometimes bad, sometimes good, but never impossible. The present fashion of writers is different. You may meet with living men and women of the nineteenth century—murderers, bigamists, poisoners, to be sure : but I shall direct my grandchildren to go

elsewhere than to the novels of the present day,
if they want to form a correct estimate of the
society in which their grandfather moved. Not
that I would have my readers by any means to
imagine that what I write has positively taken
place : I desire neither to detract from my own
reputation as an inventor, nor from the reputation
of society, as it is, by pretending to represent
even the outlines of a family history. I shall be
happy to travel within the probabilities of ordinary life; taking an exceptional case here and
there, and making the conduct of my *dramatis
personæ* consistent with their education, temperament, circumstances, or temptations. It will give
me no pleasure to turn round upon my critic and
declare that facts are true and authentic, when
the characteristics of my actors do not lead up to
an inference of my facts.

Do not flatter yourself therefore, my friend,
that you are Harold Falcon ; or that you or I ever
knew him in the flesh. I may know his type, so
may you ; you may yourself be he, for what I
know or care. I hope you are ; there are worse
men and better. I hope still more that you have
avoided his vices, and clung to his virtues ; for
he saw the error of his ways before he died, and
lived cleanly.

But just now we have to do with his early
life; with his introduction to Bernhard Jansen,
which can hardly imply ecclesiastical asceticism.
I mean, of course, the asceticism of the ———
party.   He came from Eton young, having
neither father nor mother; only an aristocratic,
high-minded, middle-aged, fox-hunting peer for a
guardian, who had four boys and one girl of his
own to look after.   He spent his best days at
Hawkestone Castle, with his cousin Hawkestone,
and the young Falcons, older and about the same
age as himself.   Lady Helen was the youngest,
but what with absence and the governess, he
saw little enough of her.   There was his younger
cousin George too, and a sister of his own.   They
were all at the castle, and all welcome to whatever
the castle afforded—ponies, horses, dogs, keepers,
claret, books, pocket-money, and the run of their
teeth.

When he left Eton, he left behind him a remarkable character, not so much with the masters
as with his school-fellows and the old camp-
followers of the school.   He had all along seen
that any acquaintance he might make with the
masters would cease with his school-days, while
the others were to last him his life.   He was a
great favourite, and possessed of exactly those

qualities which were likely to make him so.

Every hero ought to be a great man if he be not a good one; and there is a great difference between the two. A hero who is neither the one nor the other, should at least have some of the characteristics of greatness or goodness. Harold Falcon had one of these at all events. He possessed a recklessness and a courage which made him many admirers if they produced fewer imitators. Perhaps it is as well that this latter was the case. An anecdote at each epoch of his early life will be sufficient to convince the reader that whatever he became as a man he was a remarkable boy. It was Harold Falcon who was caught smoking, when that virtue was rarer than it has become since, and upon being questioned by the celebrated Dr Keate, assured him that it was for corns. His comrades, caught like himself *flagrante delicto*, hung their heads and were silent, or replied with more truth, but less recklessness, 'nothing, sir.' His advent at the university was not that of a common man. He entered Christ Church with a terrier at his heels and a sack on his back; and within his first hour—others talk of their first term—he had assembled some choice old Etonians, for whose pleasure he drew the badger in his bed-room. Such a manifest talent for scrapes could not live under a bushel; and by the time he had won a college steeplechase or two, and had shown the dark-blue first in the inter-university steeplechase in the vale of Aylesbury, the college authorities seemed to think he had done enough to ensure him a degree somewhere else; and without proceeding to expulsion recommended Lord Falconberg to remove his nephew's name from the books. Not, as they observed parenthetically, that he could not have taken a most respectable position in the schools, but that his tastes were scarcely consistent with that future which high academical honours point to, but do not necessarily achieve. The Bench of Bishops, the Ermine, the Houses of Parliament, and the Bar, have, it is true, exhibited much and profound scholarship—the result of Eton and Harrow, Oxford and Cambridge; but those cases have been almost universally dissociated from badger-baiting and steeplechasing while *in statu pupillari;* and the only point in which we detect any similitude between the two cases, is the rather remote one of corns.

'Harold,' said Lord Falconberg, leaning back in an easy-chair in his library, while his nephew stood with his hand upon the table a little distance off, 'I've had some little difficulty, but I have succeeded, at the War Office, and you are gazetted to the Fusileer Guards. Hawkestone wished it, and so did you; so I pressed it.' Lord Hawkestone was his eldest son.

'I'm sorry you found any difficulty; there ought to have been none.'

'Certainly there ought to have been none, considering what this Government owes to our family; I don't know that there would have been but for that foolish escapade of yours—'

'No great harm hunting the drag or driving the Tally-ho, uncle,' said Harold, sitting quietly down, as if to argue the point.

No great harm in driving it, the harm was in upsetting it. You'll find, Harold, that in the profession you're entering, bad luck is a very great fault; and you seem to me to have had your share. According to your own account, you've scarcely ever been guilty without being found out.' Here the peer smiled good-humouredly, as if he were inclined to look very lightly on the peccadillos in question.

After a few minutes' pause, in which Lord Falconberg seemed to be collecting his ideas, or rather his language for giving them expression, he resumed the very unusual task he had set himself of giving advice.

'No man alive, my dear Harold, ever attained greater success in his profession than your poor father. If an ample income, derived from several patent offices and sinecures, which he managed far to exceed, was any proof of this, there could be no doubt of it. He was an excellent soldier. There's nothing to be done without discipline ; and of all things beware of debt.' It occurred to Harold that perhaps if his uncle and he were to change places the peer might better appreciate his own advice. 'You will have temptations to surmount, as all men with your limited means must have. Eton and Oxford ought to have given you some insight into such matters.'

'I think they have, sir,' said Harold, who felt that he was expected to say something. 'I think they have ;' and he could not help smiling at the conceit.

'The regiment is not necessarily an expensive one. You can live almost as you like. Make what use you can of Grosvenor-square in the season, and get some convenient rooms in St James'-street or Pall-mall. Your poor father's income of course went with him. His life insurance and the few thousands he left behind him will be equally divided between you and Adelaide ; and as I shall continue the allowance I have hitherto made of a couple of hundreds a-year, you may with strict economy do very well. Whenever you get away you'll always find a home here.' And then the peer thought he had almost exhausted his topics of advice and counsel, so Harold thanked his uncle for the substantial assistance he promised him.

'And when am I to join, sir?'

'Oh, not immediately. Hawkestone will be down to-morrow, and then you can consult him; he'll tell you when to go to the Duke's levée, and help you in any way, except in lending you money. There never was such a fellow as that to overdraw. Whatever you do, Harold, avoid debt, and never buy a horse with calf-knees—they are sure to come to grief sooner or later.' Saying which the good-humoured old peer rose and led the way to the stables. 'Now I'll show you Lady Helen's hack. She'll be home from Paris for good in a fortnight, and I mean to surprise her.'

And so Harold Falcon got over his university difficulties, and found himself in the Scotch Fusileers, in which regiment his cousin Lord Hawkestone was senior lieutenant and captain, and a most irreproachable young officer, with the exception of that one capacity for overdrawing his allowance by some hundreds, which in his case was a matter of very little importance.

We have seen that upon two other important

occasions Harold Falcon was by no means indebted to his position in society for the eminence he attained at once ; neither did he seem inclined to shine by borrowed light in his new occupation. It was scarcely known that a cousin of Hawkestone's had joined; he had hardly been seen on the steps of the Guards' club, or at St James's, before he came rather prominently before the British public, and especially the sporting part of it, as the winner of the Liverpool. Now this was a rather high pedestal to have perched on for the practice of economy and self-denial ; the more so as his brother officers were quite ready to acknowledge the reflected glory by every mark of popularity. The winner of the Liverpool, who has graduated nowhere in horseflesh but in the provinces or at a university, must be a genius. And Byron himself could hardly have woke and found himself more famous than Harold Falcon on the day after the Liverpool. If there was any doubt about it, it soon ceased ; for he stated at breakfast in the club on the following morning, with a simplicity only to be found in an embryo guardsman, that he had given seven hundred for the winner immediately after the race; and was going to try to borrow the money to pay for him.

To those who know the value of money under the circumstances, it will not be necessary to say

how much Harold Falcon paid for it. He and
some of his friends called it ten per cent., but as
it was borrowed only for three months we shall
call it what it was—forty. 'And very fair too,'
said the discounters, who knew all about him,
'he'll have ten thousand when he comes of age, his
pay—on which he can't live—and two hundred a-
year from the peer. He's lucky to get it at all.'
And so he was; and nothing but his extraordinary
good looks, which made an impression on that
gigantic middleman, Bernhard Jansen, who was
looking about for high-class paper, got him the
money. With a winner of the Liverpool, a talent
for steering him, and a necessity for getting
money without his uncle's knowledge, if possible,
it is not remarkable that in a few years, the time
in fact at which we have arrived, Harold Falcon
had got through his little fortune, and could have
paved Pall-mall with his acceptances. Somehow or other Lord Falconberg's words had something in them. Luck was a great thing in the
profession; and Harold always lit on his feet.
Something came off the day before the little bill
was due, and then he paid a portion and renewed.
The women said, what a pity the handsomest man
in London was such a pauper; and the men said,
'the best fellows always went to the devil first.'

CHAPTER V.

MUST WIN A POT O' MONEY.

The Holt was a fine old place, about a mile from Waterpark. Large, grand, dingy, and badly furnished, save in the matter of old-fashioned sofas and modern arm-chairs. It is curious to remark how far we excel the ancients in the latter article of comfort, and their superiority to us in the former; deep-seated, large, luxurious; a sofa as big as a bed; and not a couch. I don't mean to say that a newly-furnished London drawing-room in a third-rate house, or a semi-detached villa about Pimlico, would not be spoilt by the introduction of this rare luxury, behind and beneath which children may play at hide and seek, or which—*O tempora, O mores!*—might serve to shelter more important sinners if the world be as bad as it is reported to be by those who profess to know it. It (the sofa I mean, not the world) would either put to the blush the modest blue-and-silver trumpery which does duty for

fashion at a cheap rate (twelve and sixpence in
he pound), or it would look so like a bull in a
china-shop as to ensure immediate rejection.
There wasn't a room in the Holt that had not one
or more of them, drawn up alongside of the ample
dogs and huge fireplaces, or at the foot of the
large comfortable old bedsteads, with their cherubs
and crowns and coronets in polished oak, which
frightened the wicked and the timid, when the
lurid glare of their flickering fire shone upon
them at midnight. The Holt was a pure bache-
lor's house at present. Every room in it might
have had a new carpet. Not one excepting the
drawing-room but exhibited symptoms of shooting boots, dog's victuals, and cigar ashes, and—
horresco referens—the bed-rooms themselves smelt
of smoke.

After this description of the house you will
scarcely want to go as far as the stables. You
will be wrong. In those three sides of a quadrangle you will see all the lavish expense of the
owner. The interior has all the cleanliness and
decoration which Benedict would have given to
the house. Not a luxury is wanting that can be
obtained with due regard to ventilation and health.
No smoking there ; it's a rule of the place. The
property is too valuable to be burnt. Whether

or no the same estimate is attached to the ancestors that decorate the walls, amidst the valuable
Angelos, Caraccis, Poussins, and Carlo Dolces,
the heir-looms of a long and wealthy line, I can't
say ; but it is quite clear that the risk may be run.
I believe, if no sense of shame withheld the avowal,
that Dick Carruthers would prefer to see the
whole house in flames, as long as nobody was in
it, to the smallest accident to some half-dozen of
the tenants of those loose boxes. He knows all
the pictures, he says, and he never means to look
into one of the books ; while he enjoys a fresh
pleasure every time he gets on to the back of
any one of his horses, and wins more money
pretty nearly every time he sees them run.

If a lady is honouring me by reading this
book, I can forgive her curiosity to know something more of Dick Carruthers. It is but natural
that she should like to analyze the Dick Carruthers of this wicked world with a view to avoid
them. No man need want to know much about
him ; there are plenty more where he came from.

He was a man of large fortune, old family,
without more education than was to be picked up
accidentally at a public school. He was what you
or I should have called 'a good fellow,' if we
knew him a little : if we went to stay with him

once a year, for example, to shoot his covers or to
ride—well, no, not unless he was well assured of
your capability. He was fond of filling his house
at certain times, and with certain men, because *he*
liked it, without much reference to them. If you
didn't want a dinner, and were quite capable of
appreciating a good one, he would be most happy
to see you; and if you had half-a-dozen houses to
go to, and very large studs at your command, he
would bore you to come to him, and ride his
horses. But if you wanted a dinner, or if you
would like to have stayed with him for change of
air, or rest, or health, he certainly would not have
cared to ask you. If you were a poor devil, fond
of hunting, without a horse to ride, Dick Carruthers would have recommended you to go to—
Tollitt. There are plenty of men, different from
this, who like helping the lame, blind, halt, and
needy; and I have the pleasure of their acquaintance and enjoy it. I hope they'll accept of this
handsome acknowledgment: but there are plenty
of the other sort too, who sail through the world
under the name of 'good fellows,' 'capital fellows,' 'first-rate fellows,' and Dick Carruthers was
one of them: but he's nothing to do with the
story. Let's see who he had in the house that has.

'Who's coming to dinner to-day, Dick?' said

Harold Falcon, as they sauntered across the hall, and saw the preparations going on through an open door.

'Loxton and Dashwood, and an Oxford man, Beauchamp, whom you don't know. Johnson,' said the master of the house, calling to the butler as he crossed the hall, 'how many have we at table to-day?'

'Only eleven, sir. We have laid for twelve, but it's one too many.'

'Ask that unfortunate curate, Dick,' says Harold; 'he'll enjoy it.'

'What's the use of asking him? he won't amuse us much,' replies the master.

'Perhaps we shall amuse him,' says the other; 'he'll enjoy a good dinner and a bottle of your claret after it. I dare say he's been at work in the parish all day long, and would be glad of the change.'

'He won't play at loo nor at pool, at least not for money, and he won't lay the odds nor take them; and he never heard of the Rover, so I don't see what use he'll be to us.' This argument was decisive, and as it wasn't Harold Falcon's house nor dinner, he said no more.

'I'll tell you what we'll do after luncheon, Falcon; we'll get Armitage to ride with us over to Longford, and ask the rector to dinner : he's the best judge of claret in the county, and he says that '34 of mine will be quite first-rate.' Harold acquiesced of course, and asked what they were to ride.

'You shall have out the Rover, he wants a little schooling; and we'll put Armitage on the chestnut mare. He's sure to come to grief; but it will do them both good:' with which considerate speech and intention for his guests' comfort, the best fellow in the world went back to the stable to give his orders, and Harold Falcon went into the library to look at the odds for the Waterpark handicap.

To the intense disappointment of Dick and his friends, the chestnut was only down twice in the excursion, and Armitage was not hurt either time. The Rover fenced as brilliantly as usual, and looked all that could be desired by his backers.

The rector of Longford, a good sort of man, who might rather be called a black squire, accepted the invitation which was given him : and he belied neither the soundness of the claret nor of his own constitution, when his dog-cart was ordered at half-past eleven to carry him back to his home.

We write of a time when smoking was not what it is now. I had never seen a gentleman with a pipe at that time : and the nearest approach to it was the remnant of the parsons Adams or Trulliber, as exhibited in a Welsh curate. Cigars were admissible at the Universities and in bachelors' houses ; and some few large and very commodious country-seats boasted a proper smoking-room. Had any one, even at Dick Carruthers', then told me that I should live to see the colouring of meerschaums the principal occupation of our young men, I should have believed in it much as I should have believed that a morning visit could be paid in Grosvenor-square in a shooting jacket and a felt hat.

But inasmuch as smoking was not such a business then as now, it was more of a pleasure ; and the men who did smoke enjoyed the luxury with a gusto as superior as that of the moderate claret drinker to the indiscriminate toper of all kinds of poison. Nay, I can hardly hesitate to say that the tobacco was better and the appreciation of it juster. For as the amiable youth, who leaves a lower form at Eton to finish that education which has never yet been begun, furnishes himself openly with regalias at ninepence, and cabanas at sixpence a piece, it is difficult to believe that such a temptation to plunder can be resisted. The British merchant is, as we know, proof against much; but, unless it be from the heads of the profession, such a box of cigars as perfumed the billiard-room at the Holt on the evening in question, is seldom produced in these degenerate days.

'How did the horse go to-day, Falcon?' says young Dashwood of the Fourth Dragoon Guards, chalking his cue and proceeding to hole his adversary in the middle pocket.

'Have you backed him yet?' replies Harold Falcon.

'Not for a halfpenny. Game; that's another fiver,' upon which Lord Farrington, with a readiness which did him credit, instead of taking it, handed over a ten pound note, and resigned his cue.

'The sooner you do so the better. He was at seven to one, now he's at four, and he may be at evens before they start,' again says Falcon.

'We have heard of the fox and his brush. You have backed him yourself.'

'I have: and if you want an opinion of his merits, I can give an honest one: for I rode him to-day. I believe he'll win. He's very fast, and nothing but a sheer accident can get him down.'

'How many are going for the steeplechase?' inquires Sir Harry Armitage.

'There are six or seven likely to start; but no one knows till the day. He's thorough-bred; and the chances are that none of the others are so.'

'I believe he'll win, if he remains all right,' remarks Dick Carruthers, who has taken apparently little interest in the conversation. 'He can give anything in the stable, two stone at least: and he has just time to be leisurely and carefully prepared.'

'Then back him yourself, Dick,' calls out Farrington from the other end of the room, where he was lounging; for the discussion about the Rover had put an end to the billiards for the time. 'Back him yourself, and then we shall know you're in earnest.'

'So I will at four to one, if any one will make it worth my while: I'll do it to a thousand.' Nobody immediately responded, and one or two laughed.

'The odds are a little long, Carruthers,' said Harold, 'but I'll do it; I can afford it. I'll lay you four thousand to one: book it.' And Harold Falcon took from the pocket of his dress-coat the inevitable betting-book.

'Hang it, Harold,' said Farrington again; 'that's heavy betting.'

'Not too heavy—I'll have a run for my money at any rate. I took seven thousand to one myself—so I stand to win there to nothing, at all events. I don't think that beggar Carruthers meant anything,' said Falcon, laughing good-humouredly, 'but we've nailed him now.' The expression of surprise on the faces of most of Dick's guests was marvellous: and knowing Harold Falcon's general impecuniosity they were not prepared for such a wager. However, the bet was booked, and there was an end of the business.

'Is that your cousin at T——? There's one of your family up there whom I know very well,' said Beauchamp, turning suddenly to Harold Falcon: a tall, thin, rather light man. And he was proceeding to give further details, when Harold interrupted him good-humouredly.

'Yes: never mind about saying how ill-favoured he is—that's my cousin—not much of the family-cut about him. What does he do—read?'

'Just now he's said to be very spoony on a girl they call Peggy Jansen.'

'Just the sort of fellow that would be spoony

on Peggy Jansen,' says Harold Falcon, 'isn't he, Farrington?'

'What! do you know Peggy Jansen?' says Beauchamp, opening his eyes with astonishment.

'Of course I do—her father's a most respectable man, and a great friend of mine.' Here the rest, who were already initiated in the mysteries of bill-discounting and Bernhard Jansen, laughed. 'I'm glad George didn't see me lay four thousand to one against the Rover.'

'Why so?' said two or three at once, Beauchamp among them.

'Because he's fond of money, and it might upset him to think of so much good credit going out of the family coffers. I don't like to call it hard cash.'

CHAPTER VI.

JANSEN'S HOUSEHOLD ARRANGEMENTS.

THE interior of the farm-house near Woodstock, in which Jansen and his wife and daughter
lived, was remarkable externally and internally.
Its gable ends and peculiarity of building, without any settled design or order, the black-coloured
rafters and beams which ran along it through the
red bricks, crossing them and supporting each
other, with the wooden eaves which overhung
the ground story, made it eminently picturesque.
It wanted however in comfort whatever it gained
in appearance inside and out. It was not so
much the neglect of poverty as of indifference.
No attempt was made, though the winter was passing away, to train the creepers which hung in
wild luxuriance over its door and windows. The
grass was uncared-for, excepting by a single
goat, who, tethered by a cord, was attempting to
keep down the grass-plot: and the last year's

beds seemed to be much in the state in which a
northern autumn was likely to have left them.

Inside affairs were only so far different, that
as in this climate we live in-doors and not out,
personal necessities demand some provision of
warmth. The square old hall, paved, not boarded,
was uneven and broken ; the room on the right,
a large, square, well-shaped chamber, panelled
and dark, was used as a workshop : it contained
at present a long carpenter's table or settle; a
variety of tools, and coloured woods fit for working, and some splendid models of carved birds
and flowers. The room was simply whitewashed
as to its ceiling and wall above the oaken wain-
scot. It contained, however, some very extraordinary curiosities in the way of clocks, toys,
and automata, besides fine old specimens of carving in various woods and styles. There were,
too, some valuable pictures, but all by Dutch
masters ; and some of them were family portraits,
burgomeisters and city dignities, who would have
shamed—with their fur cloaks, gold chains, and
magnificent beards—the lord-mayors and com-
mon-councilmen of the greatest commercial city
in the world. They stand in need of a flattering
Holbein, Vandyck, or Rubens to bring them up
to the mark of old Bernhard Jansen's ancestors ;

for such they were said to be. There was no
attempt at hanging them now, though it was
reported that some had undergone that process
in more perilous times, when Horn and Egmont
suffered too. There they stood leaning up against
the wall, or propped against a chair which would
certainly not have borne their living represent-
atives.

Had you visited every room in the house but
one, and that was his daughter Margaret's room,
you would have seen much the same sort of thing;
for a Nuremberg life and the peculiarities of her
husband's occupation, had made Dame Jansen
very indifferent to English tidiness; and she
picked her way among the broken furniture with
as much ease as Herr Jansen knocked it down.

But there was one curiosity in the room
greater than any other there, and this was Bernhard Jansen himself. He was sitting away from
the fire-place, which was well filled with a mixture
of wood and coal. His coat was off, as though he
had been engaged in his occupation; and his
huge frame was resting easily in a large and comfortable arm-chair. He was smoking a German
pipe of painted porcelain, of some value, and of
a size to match himself. At his right-hand was
a long-necked bottle of excellent Schiedam, a

tumbler, and sugar basin of silver of antique pattern, and a jug of boiling water stood near. He was engaged in looking over a betting-book. We have already spoken of his size : he was a handsome man, in many respects, too. His eyes were large and bright, though overshadowed with thick brows, and the lower part of his face was almost concealed by a drooping moustache and a long, silky, and venerable beard. In the present day this would not have been as remarkable as it was then.

The door opened, and a tall, meagre-looking woman of about forty-three or four years of age entered the room. Her features, too, were straight and good, but not pleasant to look upon. The light was waning, as it was nearly half-past five. The Frau rested a moment on the threshold of the door, and then advanced into the room.

'Mrs Jansen,' said the occupant, emitting a cloud of very fragrant tobacco, but looking sternly up from the book, in which he was calculating, not bets, but the dates of discounted bills, 'the tea is not ready yet.'

'That's no reason why you should be drinking hot Hollands-and-water at this time;' for it was a remarkable fact that Frau Jansen made a point of increasing her own ill-humour to match that of her husband: having begun life with a little the best of it in that respect, she had too much self-respect ever to lose caste.

'I drink what I like,' replied he, knitting his brows.

'Say, rather, you like what you drink. I should think, Giant, you've made it too strong of the lemon, by your temper.' Giant was not so much a term of endearment as it first appears to be. It was something between 'Bernhard' and 'you old fool,' and could be turned either to one or the other at a moment's notice. Herr Jansen continued to smoke in silence.

'I thought how it would be when Peggy was gone.'

'As far as the girl is concerned it would be a good thing if she was never to come back again. Look at that.' And here Herr Jansen held out a letter to his wife; which she read and returned to him.

'And where did this come from?' said she, after a moment's hesitation.

'From that precious glover, who's making a sale of her own daughters, and would be glad to send yours to the same market.'

'Hoity toity.' And here in strong emotion, be it remarked, Frau Jansen became as English as she had been twenty years ago. 'I suppose you mean you interfered as usual just at the wrong time. If you expect to marry your daughter respectably by sending her away every time a gentleman says or writes a civil word to her—'

'Civil word, *donner wetter!* Frau Jansen,' and here the Giant struck his fist violently on the table, shaking everything in the room but his wife's nerves, 'do you call this G. F.'s (whoever he is) civil words? Doesn't he ask her to meet him without the knowledge of her father or her mother? Is that the English for civil words, Frau Jansen: for if so, I like better the language of my own country. It wasn't the way I asked you to be my wife. Do you know who this G. F., as he calls himself, is?' And then he held out the note once more, flattening it for his wife's perusal with his other hand.

'Do I know? of course I do. But the man's in such a hurry, there is no doing or saying anything.' And the Frau turned round, and opening her hands, appealed to the other curiosities of the room. 'Has she a secret from her mother, do you think? And now, when matters were beginning to take a turn, hey, presto! she's gone. Send for her back, and beg her pardon for your suspicions.' This was a long speech and a cunning one, but Herr

Jansen was not to be turned from his former question.

'Who is this G. F. ? Yes, Frau Jansen,—this G. F. whom I heard talking to our Peggy on the other side of our wall ? Would that I could have caught him. I tell you, woman, they did talk of marriage; but it was she, not he.' The fact is that Bernhard Jansen had heard that evening more than was good for him, yet not quite enough.

'Then, stupid, I tell you who the G. F. you speak of is—he is George Fellowes; he is what you call edel, noble; but we don't overrun our country with small nobility, we are satisfied with gentlemen, Edelmänner. Will not that do for your daughter ?'

'Honestly, Mrs Jansen, it will. And when such an one comes to carry off my lamb, he will come by the door of the sheepfold. He'll not climb over the wrong way. If he does, he'll meet the fate of the wolf. You understand ?'

'Good,' replied the woman; 'let her marry whom she will, only let her love him. That won't be one of your workmen—artisans. She has not been taught to love such, Herr Jansen. You have never taught her to love such. You wouldn't like to mend chairs and tables, no more will she.'

'Love, did I say love ? No! I said marriage.
If this Fellowes will marry her—well: but I
know him better. However, she is gone for the
present, and until these boys return to their
homes, she must remain away. She shall come
no more into temptation.'

'Temptation; listen to me. You have told
me of your blood; your ancestors, look at them.
Shall your daughter marry beneath them. They
were great men in Holland and in Germany. She
has beauty, learning, wit (of which, indeed, she
had none). You have ambition for her, Giant.
Leave her to me.'

The giant mixed himself more grog, and forgot his tea. He held his tongue, for in truth, he
thought to a certain extent with his wife, but he
had his reasonable fears. His open nature was
more than a match for his wife's worldliness.
Bernhard Jansen would have liked his daughter
to have married a gentleman. He had seen some
of all sorts, and he knew Peggy to be unfitted
for the life of an artisan, even were he one of his
own class. Besides, he knew what his wife did
not; that there was a little money, a thousand or
two even, to go with her. A relation had left
it her, and he had improved it; and in all his
difficulties he had never diminished what he

called Peggy's fortune. At all events she was out of harm's way now at a cousin's house in Scotland, who was well-to-do in the world; and though he wanted his daughter, he would keep her there till the wolf, as he chose to call him, was away from the neighbourhood.

He was still in a brown study; his wife held her tongue, and candles had been brought him by their single maid-servant. Frau Jansen pretended to sleep and allowed the Hollands and pipe to do duty for tea. Just then a horse came into the old court-yard, and a man's voice inquired for Mr Jansen. The master put on his coat and went out.

'Ah, ah, Mr Falcon—you—so late? What is it now?' said he, ushering into the room our old acquaintance Harold Falcon.

'The old story, Jansen. Money. I must have money, and at once.'

'Money is scarce: besides, that last bill—'

'Shall be paid, Jansen—it is due next week; but I must have five hundred to-morrow at latest.'

'And the names?'

'Good, my own and Lord Barthefield,' replied Harold.

'And the percentage?' said Jansen, not disposed to make difficulties with so good a customer as Harold had hitherto proved.

'Shall be as before—three months only—I shall be in funds.'

'Then give me your acceptance for six hundred; but you must give me time to send to London. The day after to-morrow, Captain.'

'Good. I may depend upon it.' And Harold rode rapidly out of the yard towards Oxford. When Frau Jansen heard who the visitor was, she said, 'There, Giant, why don't you do something of that sort for Peggy?'

'Peggy, by heaven, it shall be. Frau Jansen is right.' And Herr Jansen began to think in earnest. But first he lit another pipe.

CHAPTER VII.

THE COUSINS.

HAROLD FALCON lost no time on the Woodstock road; and, indeed, his horse was not inclined to let him. He was an Oxford hack, and
knew the road and the pace he was expected to
go. It's an honest, good animal, or was in those
days, so long as he was well fed, but possibly he
may have degenerated. When we have a poor
man's college or a nonconformist hall, he ought
to go out altogether in compliment to the new
comers. At present he only finds himself a little
de trop from the able use that undergraduates are
learning to make of their own legs. Well, it is
cheaper at all events, and I have become a father
since those days. I have changed sides.

When Harold reached Oxford, having left his
horse at the stables, he walked into T—— College,
and through the gate, which was still open. The
porter was standing on the steps of his *conciergerie*,
and Harold asked if Mr Falcon was in his rooms.

'Yes, sir,' said Walker, grinning facetiously.
He's in his rooms ; glad to be the first to tell you
the news.   Your cousin got his ' testamur' yesterday, sir ; there was only one of us plucked, sir,
and we've nineteen going for honours.   They do
say there'll be two firsts quite certain, and I am
told they'll give Mr Falcon a honorary fourth.
But there's nothing so uncertain as a honorary
fourth.   I've seen more gents disappointed over
a fourth than over anythink.   There was Mr
Jenkins, now, of course he never read, but he
was—' By this time Harold had got half-a-sove-
reign out of his pocket, which it was clear that
old Walker coveted, if he did not deserve, and
which saved him the melancholy rehearsal of
Jenkins' talents and disappointment.   'Thankye,
sir,' said the old man, putting it away in his
waistcoat pocket that it might not mingle with
the half-crowns and shillings he had already received; 'thankye, sir; I'm sure I hope Master
George will get a fourth, for we think a deal
more of it than a second or a third.   It's almost
as good as a first, only the president don't care
so much about it, cos it don't look so well on the
list,' by which time Harold was out of earshot and
nearing his cousin's rooms.

He found George Falcon preparing for the re-

ception of a supper party. As might have been
expected, learning was at so low an ebb that its
most ordinary exhibition was about to be celebrated by a splendid entertainment. George was
about to celebrate his success by the most barbarous
of festivals. In another hour it was at its height.
An apology is always due to the reader for an
introduction of an Oxford supper party; not only
has it been done *ad nauseam,* but it is so little
worth doing that I shall make but short work of it.
Christ Church and Merton sent each its contin-
gent; and a few of his most intimate associates
from his own college made up some sixteen or
eighteen guests. Flat deal slabs of ready-opened
oysters preceded the heavier viands; cold turkeys,
chickens, ham, tongues, and pressed beef, with
a fair assortment of jellies and sweetmeats,
tempted carnivorous appetites that had only
dined about four hours before; champagne, and
huge jorums of bishop, cardinal, egg-flip, and
punch were waiting to be consumed. The table
groaned, but the guests were not yet arrived.
The supper was as refined as the conversation
was likely to be. Who has not assisted at some
such uncivilized rites, and who does not wonder
at his own stupidity? The only thing not to
wonder at in the whole performance is the head-

ache of the following morning. George welcomed his cousin with a nod, as he decantered some sherry.

'I congratulate you, George, and myself too.'

'On what?'

'You on your examination, and myself on having arrived before the savages, who are evidently expected.' George Falcon laughed, and his cousin continued, 'I wanted two or three minutes' chat with you.'

'You can have it. Nothing very serious, I presume.'

'Well, not particularly so; it might have been worse.'

'Then you can stay to supper, and we can talk over the other business to-morrow morning,' said George, who added, parenthetically, 'D— that scout of mine, he's always losing the corkscrew,' which was, and is, and will be true of all scouts, past, present, and to come.

'No, I can't do that; I've not dined yet, and you will be quite unfitted for business to-morrow; let's have it out now, and I'll go to the 'Mitre' to dinner.'

'Where did you come from, Harold?'

'Last from Woodstock. I rode one of Carruthers' horses from Waterpark this afternoon, and Seckham sent over a hack to meet me. A very good one he was.'

The candles were not yet lit, and the room, which was large and lofty, continued in partial darkness, or a change in George Falcon's features, at the mention of Woodstock, might have been perceptible. He remembered that Harold had been seen there, unaccountably, once or twice before.

'Woodstock; that's not the shortest way.'

'There's not much difference, but I wanted to see some one.'

'I should have thought your acquaintance in that neighbourhood was small.'

'I wanted to see a man of the name of Jansen.' George Falcon now really lost his presence of mind, and looked up at his cousin wonderingly.

'And what could you want with Jansen? he lives out of Woodstock.'

'Just what I want with you now.'

'But who is Jansen?' said George, feeling that he had committed himself a little and anxious to retrieve the false step.

'If you don't know, George,' replied the other in a bantering way, 'it's as well you shouldn't make his acquaintance.'

'But I want to know. I've heard men speak of him.'

' You mean of his daughter, don't you ? ' and if Harold could have seen his cousin's face now, he might have resisted the pleasure of any further banter. ' I hear you're spoony in that quarter. It's a dangerous state for an undergraduate; however, I presume you've done with the university now for some time.'

' I shall come up to keep my master's— : and now tell me what you want with me, as you won't stop to supper.'

' I want you to lend me a hundred pounds to-night. Give me a check.'

' Money's scarce,' said George, unconsciously buttoning his pocket. We didn't wear long slits in those days.

' Just the very words old Jansen said. You can have it back again the day after to-morrow. The fact is I'm on my way to Borodaile's, and I can't go without it. There's not another man in the university with as much, I should think; that's why I came to you.'

' What's it worth to you, Harold ? ' said the other with a cold sneer.

' It may be worth a good deal or not, that's as luck goes; but I'll give you a hundred and twenty for it the day after to-morrow.'

George hesitated still, not that he really intended to refuse, but he could not part with a promise without some reluctance.

'There, never mind about calculating the percentage. Old Jansen would do it for less. I didn't see his daughter to-day; but—by Jove, I nearly forgot—as I was coming away I undertook to get a letter delivered to one George Fellowes. Old Jansen didn't know what College, but I said I'd get it done for him. I suppose George Fellowes has been getting up behind a piece of paper. Do you know him, George?' Harold did not notice George's face now, or he might have been surprised by its pained and astonished look, while holding out his hand he said with great rapidity, 'Yes, yes. I'll undertake that he gets it—it is money-matters of course,'—and taking the letter he thrust it rapidly into his pocket.

'That's all right. I don't suppose you do much in that way. Now give me a piece of paper. There: I.O.U. one hundred and twenty pounds. Accidents may happen, and you wouldn't have much to fight over, if I was to go, George. I don't suppose Adelaide would care, but I should feel quite unhappy at your disappointment.'

George Falcon wrote a cheque for a hundred pounds almost mechanically, and put the other into his pocket. It served to balance the weight of the letter to George Fellowes.

The moment his cousin left the room, he drew out the letter and tore it open; it was simple and easily comprehensible.

'SIR,

'Your attentions to my daughter are understood, and your last letter has been received. Both are estimated at their true value. It will be better for you that you should not be found in her company, or on my premises.

'Your obedient servant,
'BERNHARD JANSEN.'

George Falcon read these few lines a second time; an angry flush came to his face, and then it turned pale as the gray ashes into which he threw the note.

His cousin Harold walked down to the 'Mitre,' whither he had sent his clothes beforehand, ordered a little dinner, walked into Christ Church, won thirty pounds at *Vingt et un*, and drove the Defiance the next morning to Stokenchurch Hill, where a carriage took him to his friend Lord Borodaile's. He did double the hundred his cousin George lent him, and immediately redeemed his I.O.U. for one hundred and twenty, to that cousin's delight, more than to his own astonishment.

Perhaps in disposition, as in appearance, no two men could be less alike than Harold and George Falcon. The former was of a gay, careless temperament, which reached positive recklessness; and his ruin (not difficult to accomplish, it must be admitted) had been achieved within a year or two of his purchase of the seven-hundred-guinea steeplechaser, and mainly by his attachment to that flattering animal and others of his class. George, on the contrary, was of a close unsympathizing disposition, who went into society even at an early age for what he could get, and who gamed at a time of life when others gambled. His great and leading principle was to defend himself by attacking others; and though he would have been called the most unflinching player of the playmen of his day, he was as prudent as if it had been the solemnest occupation of life. He always made acquaintances, for he expected them to be useful to him; he never made friends, lest the intimacy might be turned to his disadvantage. Harold never had an acquaintance that did not become a friend, nor a friend whom he would have hesitated to assist with his last shilling. By the time he was three-and-twenty

he had no other shilling to help them with. He
had most unbounded belief in his luck, which,
although it beggared him, and left him frequently
without a hundred pounds in the world, was always doing him a good turn at odd unexpected
times; and as he began life with but little, he
sometimes after a good week, as he called it, was
as rich as he ever had been. When he sold out,
his uncle, Lord Falconberg, was very angry, and
vowed he never would forgive him. In a month
he was at Hawkestone Castle, taking all the
trouble off his uncle's hands, and replacing
Hawkestone, who was doing duty with the regiment of which he had washed his hands. It's
very wrong of the world, but there's not a hard-
working clergyman with ten children, who falls
into debt and misery, whom his creditors fail to
assail as a spendthrift and an idler; while, if
Harold Falcon had come to grief, there's not a
man would have lodged a detainer against him.
He always conciliated the one with the money
that belonged to another. George never owed a
shilling, was as exemplary in his college life as he
had been elsewhere, and had lived on his whist
and *Vingt et un* among men who were only amus-
ing themselves by losing. Both were tall, and
looked like gentlemen. George was pale, subdued,

blue-eyed, light, and straight-haired. Harold was dark-eyed, open, laughter-loving, and handsome as the day. Their pursuits were different, and their tastes, and minds. George was slow but industrious. Harold was quick, idle, impulsive; and far the cleverer of the two. They were not fond of one another, which is not to be wondered at. Active dislike wasn't in the nature of Harold; the extent of his hostility was borrowing money, and it gave him more pleasure to get it out of George than any one else.

Just now George Falcon had another grievance against Harold. He was unable to divest his mind of the idea that his cousin was endeavouring to supplant him with Peggy Jansen. For, although he would have been glad to be relieved of an amour which was likely to give him incredible anxiety and to end in expense if not exposure, he was so happily gifted with a contrariety of disposition, that he would have hated the man who should relieve him of his trouble, if he took the innocent cause of it with him. It was a personal offence to fall in love with the same woman, when it ought to be regarded as the most delicate flattery. A man at the antipodes has surely a right to worship the sun, though all the time that luminary may be shining only upon you. Perhaps if

George Falcon had known Bernhard Jansen and his relations with his cousin and his set, he would have been quite as much disposed to attribute Harold's visits to the right cause; for he had a firm belief in the superiority of money over women, as an attraction.

But strange to say, Harold had seen and talked to Peggy Jansen; and, although his debts and difficulties had given him no time for falling in love, he had often thought that he had never seen so attractive a woman in his life. He delighted in her large, confiding blue eyes, and long lashes, the luxuriant gold of her hair, the pretty simple smile which she wore habitually, and her clear complexion, so delicate but so indicative of health. Love under such circumstances never entered his head; for it was rather much to say for a man like Harold, who led the free and easy life which he did, and who had not been brought up in the strictest school of propriety, that deliberate seduction was not amongst his vices. Admiration he had often felt and expressed to others of the money-lender's daughter; and for marriage he could only have looked to a class which, with all his good looks, in his present state of decadence, would possibly have overlooked him.

CHAPTER VIII.

WHO RIDES THE ROVER?

TIME went steadily on, with Harold Falcon
more quietly than usual; for having all sorts of
bills out at all sorts of dates, it very seldom happened that there was not some pleasant anticipation to quicken the flagging hours.   One acceptance for a thousand at six months, and another
for six hundred at nine, makes three-fourths of
the year go uncommonly fast; and as Christmas
approaches, the fourth quarter follows suit, bringing with it those reminiscences which are never
so agreeable as when accompanied by a favourable balance at your banker's.   Harold was sometimes dull, when he wondered what was to be
the end of a career, which seemed already to have
arrived, and the end of the world, as far as he
was concerned, to be resisted only by Bernhard
Jansen and the bill-discounters.   But he was
never impatient; for he always reflected that in

a short time he should certainly want all that he was anxious to get rid of now.

His cousin George had left Oxford, so that he saw little of him. He was gone somewhere to Scotland, or on the continent, whither he didn't know. Somebody had his address at Hawkestone, but nobody seemed to know it. However, it wasn't wanted. His usual residence was in London; he found it handy for the clubs and Tattersall's, and he kept up an intimacy with his own brother-officers. When he liked he went to Hawkestone Castle, where they were all glad to see him; none more than his cousin Lady Helen, who was now permanently at home, as the mistress of her father's household. Lord Hawkestone too had just retired, for his health was not so good as it had been, and neither London nor Windsor agreed with him. Of the three younger ones, one was still at Eton, one was at Woolwich, and the other was reading with a tutor preparatory to ordination in the neighbourhood of the Castle. It was a pleasant house, generally full of company; and Lady Helen herself not the least agreeable of its inmates. There was a great intimacy between her and Harold; just the sort of intimacy which might have ripened into a warmer attachment, or which might have existed all their lives long between cousins, and defied the most censorious.

One thing rather militated against this platonic assumption, and that was the fascinations of the Lady Helen Falcon. She was one of the handsomest girls in England, with a dignity of manner and address toned down by the most natural grace. She had acquired in Paris (where she had spent a season or two with a distant relative, and one of the most highly-bred women in France) that extreme ease and polish, which is as far removed on the one hand from our national hauteur as it is from a freedom of manner and speech erroneously attributed to our neighbours. She was of a fair complexion, with hazel eyes and dark lashes, her hair was a light brown, beautifully soft and luxuriant, her nose and mouth faultless in shape, not too small to give character to her face, with a certain strength and self-government which was indicated by a somewhat *prononcé* but handsomely-shaped chin. The old gossips of Hawkestone never could understand how two such very handsome people could come together so often without falling in love; as if there were more gravitation in beauty than in ugliness; for it's all owing to the laws of gravitation after all.

It was the week before Easter; a few people were in town—not many—and Harold Falcon was among them. On the steps of a small house next door to what is now the Wellington, but which was then Crockford's, Lord Borodaile was sunning himself, while waiting for his horses.

'Hallo, Prendergast, where are you going?'

'To Dick Carruthers, to inquire after the Rover. There was a report at the club this morning that he wasn't all right.'

'Then wait a minute, old fellow, and you'll know all about it: here comes Harold Falcon. He's his principal supporter. He's coming by Herries' now. I know him at any distance. He looks as if he ought to have twenty thousand a-year. I wish he had.'

'Talking of that, they say Hawkestone's very ill—at least, in very bad health.'

'I'm afraid you're travelling a long way for the twenty thousand. The old peer has four sons, and the three last are as strong as cart-horses, and take as much care of themselves as a half-bred'un through diet. And Hawkestone has the influenza, that's all. Well, Harold, tell us the news.'

'News? Coronation's sure to win the Derby; and they're going to insist upon residence, and some strong measures of ecclesiastical reform, after the recess. Perhaps my cousin will give up his prospects in the Church,' replied Harold in a tone of great good-humour, as if he never had a care ; and if that Jamaica-coloured insurrectionist sits behind such a horseman as Harold he must have a very hard time of it over a country.

' Then you'd better go in for the family living,' said Lord Borodaile.

' They might make some unpleasant remarks about his care for the dead ones,' said Prendergast.

' No—I've no wish to emulate our friend, the Montgomeryshire handicapper, who was so tickled with his performances on two or three occasions, that he got his son made coroner for the county. At present I'm in search of the odds about the Rover,' replied Harold.

' The very horse we were talking of. It's all right, I suppose — because they were talking treason at the club.'

' Were they ? then you go and back him right royally,' said Harold.

' Where are you going to look for the odds, Falcon ? '

' At Long's ; there's half the university in

London ; and it's difficult to know whether they are only reckless, or whether they are really as ignorant as they affect to be.' This sounds almost like an anachronism for our own time.

'And who has Carruthers got to ride him ?' said Prendergast, referring to the subject once more after a pause.

'I believe that man McPulham—I don't like him much.'

'Not a good horseman?' inquired Lord Borodaile.

'Too good,' said the other; 'he can stop them when he likes.'

'Is McPulham a gentleman ?'

'So he says—at all events he's a gentleman-rider.'

'Does he get anything now for riding ?' said Prendergast.

'He says not. He's only put on so much to nothing, which answers the same purpose if he wins. When he loses, I don't know what he does. They say he looks out for himself, and leaves his backers to settle it among themselves.'

'You stand a lot of money on the horse, don't you, Falcon ? Why don't you insist upon riding yourself ?'

'He's not my horse, and Carruthers knows

McPulham can ride him well enough if he likes—
better than I can. Besides, they heard me lay
four thousand against him.'

'But they know you've taken seven.'

'You do; so does Borodaile. So do half-a-
dozen more, and I hope Cranstone hasn't forgotten
it. But there are hundreds who don't, and if the
horse made a mistake, and he's never made one
yet, I believe, you know what a nice set they are.
The layers of fifteen sovereigns to five would pull
you off your horse, while the losers of thousands
would take the earliest opportunity of inquiring
whether 'the horse is meant to-day?' There
are men who don't conceive it possible for a horse
to lose a race when they have backed him, and
who have gone on to the turf with a full assurance
that there's not an honest man, but themselves,
belonging to it. The only reason these fellows
are not rogues is that they have not brains
enough for the business.' Saying which, and
shaking an adieu with his glove to his friends,
he took his way to Dick Carruthers' house in
Piccadilly.

The truth is that Harold Falcon was not quite
satisfied with the jockey who was to ride the
Rover; and as a question of about four thousand
pounds depended upon his success, he thought it
advisable to look after the business himself.

Carruthers he knew could have no object in risk-
ing his reputation for a dead loss, for he knew
that he at least had backed his horse honestly.
But Dick was surrounded unhappily by such a
very unscrupulous lot that they would not hesitate
to sacrifice him if it would serve their purpose.

McPulham's own character was pretty well
known. He was a very superior horseman, perhaps the best in Ireland—over a country which
may be taken to include England. But if his
horsemanship was Hibernian, so was his position
in society. In Ireland he was a gentleman for
two purposes—to ride against and to fight; and
it probably was accorded him from the great love
of sport and fighting, which at that period distinguished that gem of the sea. In England, but
for this spurious reputation, he would have been
allowed to claim the position on neither grounds;
for his associates were trainers and jockeys, and
his manners and conversation belonged to the
training-ground and the stable-yard. What his
family might have been it would have been need-
less to inquire; he had no ostensible means of
living but that which he derived by his *sobriquet*
of *gentleman*-rider; and if his father had been
really a gentleman, he was most assuredly the
last of the family who had any pretension to the
name.

CHAPTER IX.

THE PARTY AT THE HOLT.

THE recess was over, and there was but one meeting before the Derby, and that was Waterpark. It was one of those which had been established some years before, when Waterpark was a small spa, the support of one physician and two livery-stablekeepers. Eventually it became fashionable; and, from sallow-cheeked Indians with dried livers, and over-fed, cart-bred carriage horses, it rejoiced, as a winter residence, in hard-riding bachelors, officers on leave, and offshoots from Oxford and Cambridge, who, from some unknown causes, preferred to spend their vacation at Waterpark. As regards these latter, the place assumed the position of the Calais or Boulogne of bankruptcy; and there wasn't a scapegrace who had been rusticated, or who wanted to keep three horses instead of one, who didn't persuade his friends that Waterpark was good for his health. A pack of hounds, of which

one killed and two or three disabled every day
was a moderate computation, gave rise to so much
competition among the visitors, that the master
suggested an annual steeplechase, of which he
was the great patron, and to which he liberally
subscribed. Whether he found this cheaper in
the end or not, I can't say; possibly not; it was
only cutting the ditch at one end with the view
of filling it up at the other; but it produced a
meeting at the conclusion of the hunting season,
which had then become one of the most fashionable
among the provincials, and has since become one
of the most important in the kingdom.

The Holt was full; and one week before the
races, the men most interested in their success,
those who had horses, and those who had bets,
and those whose vocation it is to wander about
from country-house to country-house, tame cats,
raconteurs, gentleman-jockeys, black squires, and
bon vivants, had assembled in sufficient quantities
at Dick Carruthers' hospitable board. It was
the great house of Waterpark. There was nothing within ten miles of the place as good, and
on occasions like the present it was always open.

If any man is curious about the individual
company, I refer him to the *Morning Post*, or the
Waterpark Gazette, a well-paying emanation from

the literary talent of the neighbourhood, and the defunct *Satirist*, in which the peculiarities of more than one of the party were most unsparingly held up to ridicule. Those with whom we have to do in these pages, I shall endeavour to describe as far as may be necessary for our purpose.

I said the party was a large one, and it was a sporting one. The occupations of the party not being those of the Archbishop of Canterbury, it must not appear strange that their conversation was different from that of His Grace and the Bench of Bishops; although I know that to make people talk as they do talk is not by any means the shortest road to popularity. There's nothing so flattering to others as to make your puppets talk about things they don't understand. To meet a fool even in a book should be an implied compliment to somebody.

There were twenty people at dinner. Lord Chesterton, a quiet gentlemanly person, holding office as the master of the buckhounds, was explaining the necessity and difficulty of keeping the Conservative party together, and complaining of the inefficient registration as compared with that of the large towns.

'They have sprung up so wonderfully of late years that it requires very little management on

their part to swamp the counties,' said Lord
Chesterton, who, to tell the truth, was rather
anxious to get rid of the extremely horsey conversation which took the place of every remark.
'If they could but get the right men. There
seems always a difficulty about that.'

'They should get a foxhunter or two among
them, my Lord,' said a Captain Childers—who
went by the name of Flying Childers—an Oxfordshire man.

'The foxhunters belong to us, I fancy, to a
man,' replied Lord Chesterton.

'Then let 'em try the stag,' returned the Flying Captain, amid a roar of laughter, who, however excellent to hounds, was not blessed with
quite the same knowledge of men as of country.

'I hope, Dick, I've said nothing—'

'Nothing in the world, Childers,' said the
host. 'Chesterton is unfortunately situated, and
obliged to keep a pack of staghounds for his
sins.'

'Nonsense, Cranstone,' shouted some one,
'don't be unruly. The horse can win : nobody
will lay more than three to one at all events.
McPulham knows he can win.'

'Faith, Sir Harry, I know nothing of the sort.
I know he will if my riding can make him.

Zitella's a good animal, I believe, but I never saw her go.'

'They think it's reduced to a match. What will any one lay against Cupid?' The inquiry was made by a fast cornet of cavalry.

'I'll lay you seven hundred to one,' replied the Irishman, at once pulling out a book, which seemed as well fitted to the tails of a dress-coat as to the side-pocket of a frock. 'I'll do it in fifties or hundreds.'

The cornet received a gentle kick under the table, which he had brains enough to acknowledge by holding his tongue.

'What are likely really to go for it,' said Harold Falcon at last, waking up from an apparent dream : for the conversation had got, at one end of the table, so thoroughly into the groove that it was impossible to get it out.

'Five or six at least, Captain Falcon,' replied McPulham. 'Be dad ! I'm glad to hear the Captain's not going to be one of 'em.' This was not addressed to Harold, but was said loud enough for him to hear. 'It 'ud change the odds anyhow.'

Now Falcon disliked this implied flattery, and how little like the *bonhommie* of the true Irish gentleman it was, many of our readers know.

'Who'll go to the ball on Friday? Cranstone, you'll go : and Chesterton. Falcon, are balls in your way ? '

'I'll go with great pleasure, though I'm better in the saddle than on my feet, since my accident.' He had met with one to his foot some time back.

'We'll all go : those that can't act the bear can look like the jackass,' suggested Tom Reynolds, who was allowed some latitude in vulgarity, in the strength of being considered a wit. He was only an author. Chesterton stared, and Dick Carrruthers asked if any one would take any more claret. As every one declined, he desired Falcon to help himself to the sherry, and send it round. 'Some that my grandfather imported when he was ambassador at Madrid.'

'Then, be dad ! we'll drink the ould boy's health,' exclaimed McPulham, who had already done so. 'I'm glad he left his sherry behind him. What say you, my Lord ?' Saying which Mc Pulham helped himself, and pushed the bottle to Lord Cranstone, who sat near him. The company looked up, and Carruthers thought it time to retire.

It had been remarked that Lord Cranstone, who was usually a talkative person, and singularly agreeable in society, had scarcely spoken. He had made one remark only on the subject of the horses, and had then relapsed into an almost monosyllabic conversation with his neighbour. 'Cranstone, old fellow,' said Lord Borodaile' 'you're not up to the mark.'

'Bit of a headache. What sort of a night is it?' And Cranstone went out to see.

It was the custom at the Holt, being indeed a custom much honoured in the observance to retire for the evening to the billiard-room, where men could smoke without that offence to others, of which we are not ignorant since the railway controversy has brought it prominently forward. It is undoubtedly true that, with a feeling of perfect independence, men would light a cigar in the breakfast-room, or the library, or stand five minutes smoking in any part of the house, so much latitude has always been given or taken in such houses; but men of the world never tread on their neighbours' toes, whether they hurt them or not; so, by tacit consent, there was a billiard-room to which they usually resorted. Thus it happened on the night in question, that at least two-thirds of the party had retreated thither, after running their eyes over the morning papers. The room was warm, as indeed were some of the disquisitions on the coming opera : were we to have Rubini and Grisi again ? and were Lablache and Tambarini to be forthcoming from Paris ? on the Derby horses, and the four-in-hand club, D'Orsay's hog-maned cab-horse, and Sambo Sutton and the Oxford Pet, with half-a-dozen other subjects about as intellectual.

In the middle of it all, leaving it unsettled whether Tony Fosbroke ran away with Lady Elizabeth Bouncibel, or she with him, and whether Joe Tollitt was a better light-weight coachman than Jack Bramble, Harold Falcon found the room a little hot. It was accidental on his part, not being usually observant of temperature, or of anything else which affected only his physique. To-night, however, it was different, and he sought refuge in the hall, when he wondered whether Black Diamond was like what he was represented to be, and whether the fox-hounds, which were jumping up on the clean leathers of a former Richard Carruthers, left no mark. The scarlet coats and resplendent waist-coats of Anne, and the Jacobite heroes of George I. and II., did nothing towards cooling our hero ; so he walked into a large conservatory, which opened upon the side of the hall farthest from the billiard-room, and had an egress at the other end upon the lawn and towards the shrubberies.

Harold continued to smoke his cigar as he thought over his chances of winning a few thousands on the steeplechase, which would be something more than useful to him just now; and in a rather more contemplative mood than usual, he sat himself down at the foot of one of the large orange-trees, where he could feel the cooling night-breeze which entered by a window left purposely open for the hardening of some of the plants. Harold Falcon's knowledge of the premises enabled him to find his way to this seat even in the dark.

He had not sat there many minutes when voices, as of men speaking loudly, but not suspicious of eaves-droppers, fell upon his ear. He was scarcely conscious at first of what they were saying; and when he was so, he was about to move away, when he heard something which it was not in his power to avoid listening to.

'He can be stopped only in our part of the course, in the hollow. Nobody comes down there, and if it's to be done at all, it must be done there.' The voice, or rather the accent, was unmistakable. It was McPulham.

The reply came slowly, and after a moment's consideration. 'The horse's pace is well known

here; he can give the mare a stone at least, I
hear, and a beating. The only doubt is his re-
fusing. Since I laid against him, they say he
has much improved; but with that peculiarity of
temper, I think a horseman can have no difficulty
in making him turn.' Harold did not recognize
the speaker. ' Nor in making him jump, I suppose,' said the other. 'Faith, it takes only a
little more money.' 'I think there need be no
question of that between us,' saying which the
speakers both moved on.

There could be no doubt on Harold Falcon's
mind as to the subject of this fragment of conversation. No horse could be meant but the Rover,
and no race but the one in which he was interested, as it was the only steeplechase of the
meeting. If any uncertainty could have existed,
the voice of McPulham as one of the speakers
would have cleared that up. Now who was the
other?

Harold Falcon walked straight through the
conservatory, across the hall, and into the billiard-
room, whence he had retreated some ten minutes
before. He was not much cooler, it must be admitted. He looked round the room, and he saw
that about half-a-dozen of the company were ab-
sent. Lord Borodaile was gone to bed, Lord

Chesterton was smoking, Childers was—nobody knew where, and McPulham and Lord Cranstone were the other absentees. Of course a time does come when the most inveterate smokers and billiard-players must go to bed, and at the Holt it came at last.

'Carruthers,' said Harold, with a face full of anxiety, 'let's have five words with you.'

'Certainly. Come into my room; bring your cigar, you can finish it there. Why, Harold, you look as if you had seen a ghost.'

'I wish I had. What I've seen is more material.' And then he related to his host what he had heard. Dick looked quite incredulous.

'Are you sure, Falcon? I know you're not a likely man to make a mistake, but are you sure? because you know, old fellow, this is rather a serious charge.'

'Against McPulham, it is so; but I shall not shrink from the responsibility.'

'And who was the other? You must have some sort of suspicion.'

'I don't know, Dick, and I'd rather not have any suspicions; at all events, it won't do to state them.'

'And what do you want me to do about the

horse. He's a first-rate jockey; and you know I've backed him heavily myself.'

'He mustn't ride—he can't ride—at least among English gentlemen, and you must stop him. This is one of those cases in which it's your duty, as well as interest, to interfere.'

'What am I to do with a man who came all the way from Ireland to ride for me? Because after all, Harold, it is but one man's word against another's. What excuse can I make to get rid of the man? Cranstone's the only man that's taken him up at all, and that must be mere civility, for he'd rather see him dead than riding the Rover.'

'I don't know.' And a very curious expression passed over Harold's face. 'Will you let me ride the horse myself?'

'But what am I to do with the other fellow? He'll want to fight.'

'Then let me have the fighting too. Anything's better than a row on the turf; it gets us all a bad name. I'll manage the Irishman; and as to fighting, there's only one man in the house could or need fight him after what I've heard to-night, if he were twenty Irishmen. Leave it to me.' With which Harold Falcon took his candle and his leave, and went to bed.

CHAPTER X.

A GENTLEMAN-RIDER WITHOUT A MOUNT.

I THINK there's a story of a friend of mine which
redounds more to his credit as a wit than an
honest man. He had been guilty of that unpardonable offence in the eyes of rich men, of not
paying his debts, when he was detected in the
equally unpardonable offence in the eyes of ardent
sportsmen of sleeping long into the day when he
ought to have been starting for cover. 'I can't
think,' said his friend rather irascibly, 'how a
fellow who owes so much money can sleep at all:
you've only got twenty minutes to dress and
breakfast.' 'I can't think,' replied the unfeeling
sluggard, 'how the fellows to whom I owe it can
sleep at all:' saying which he tumbled into his
bath, and wasn't drowned.

Now I don't know how an Irish gentleman
about to commit a public robbery (for I hear that
race-horses belong to you and me, just as much as
to the persons who buy them and feed them,

which seems rather odd) usually sleeps; but on the morning after the previous conversation he was still enjoying apparently peaceful slumber, when a servant brought him a note.

The note was from Harold Falcon; and simply asked for the honour of an interview of a few minutes, if possible, before Mr McPulham left his room. Having no suspicion of the motive which had prompted the request, it was readily granted; and in ten minutes' time Harold was admitted, while McPulham performed certain duties of his toilet. At the moment of our hero's arrival he was engaged in removing the crop of superfluous stubble which one night had raised upon his lip and chin: for those were times when to have ridden a race in a beard would have called down the unequivocal ridicule of the English spectators. A chimney-pot hat under the same circumstances would have been less reprehensible.

Harold apologized, and was about to beat a retreat.

Mr McPulham begged the Captain wouldn't mention it: as he wanted to see him before breakfast, he hoped he wouldn't object, &c., &c., with those natural explanations which might have been expected on either side.

'Unfortunately,' said the Captain, 'my business admits of no delay. You were to have ridden the Rover in the steeplechase to-morrow.'

'I presume,' said the jockey, turning suddenly round with one half of his face lather and the other crimson, 'you mean to say I am to ride the Rover to-morrow.'

'Certainly, unless I can persuade you to relinquish your claim on Mr Carruthers.'

'Hardly, Captain Falcon. Faith! is it in favour of yourself that I'd be asked to do so. I've money on the race, sir.'

'And I too: and unless you wish to lose it, I should recommend you to trust the Rover to me, Mr McPulham.'

McPulham turned from the glass in which he was affecting to shave, for he had been much too nervous from the beginning of the colloquy to do much in that way, and deliberately faced the speaker, placing his razor upon the dressing-table, but forgetting to remove the remains of either soap or beard.

'Will you do me the favour to explain that language, Captain Falcon?'

'It would give me pain to be obliged to do so, Mr McPulham: but if you have forgotten the conversation into which you entered last night I shall be compelled to prompt your memory.'

'Pray, sir, did Mr Carruthers send you here to insult me? because an Irish gentleman has but one answer to such insinuations.' And McPulham sat down or leant against the foot of his bed, and folding his arms waited for Harold's reply.

'Insinuations might warrant that language and attitude; but I have to prefer a direct charge against you of an intention to pull or stop in some way or other the Rover. Hear me out, sir, if you please,' said Harold, as the other rose from the bed prepared to deny it. 'You may imagine whether I shall rest in insinuations when I tell you that I was in the conservatory when you were standing outside of it last night: and the windows were open.'

'And were you the only person with talent or dishonesty enough to invent this precious story?' for McPulham had quite brains enough to know that one man's word is as good as another practically, if not morally.

'Two persons, sir, were auditors of your conversation: we know in what part of the course your intended fraud was to have been practised, and it shall be frustrated.' McPulham had lost all courage and all colour, and sat gloomily and sulkily upon the bed. However, it was necessary to say something.

'That's not language, sir, to address to an Irish gentleman.'

'It never would have been addressed to a gentleman of any country, sir,' replied Harold, whose natural prejudice was increased to an unwonted extent by the confirmation of his suspicions. 'If Mr Carruthers were to publish this morning what he knows of your conversation last night, there's not a man in the house would sit down to breakfast with you: and as to any countenance in a meeting to which your own language points, I don't know what may be the customs of your country, or for what purposes a man may be considered to rank as a gentleman: I can only tell you that in this, the less that is said of such a business the better. I shall be especially cautious in my remarks, and I can answer for the other recipient of your intentions not betraying you. I pledge you my honour for both of us; but my advice is that you retire as soon as possible: you may be quite certain that your apology will be accepted by Mr Carruthers, and that a jockey will be found to supply your place for to-morrow—if not so accomplished a horseman, at least capable of winning on such a horse as the Rover.' Saying which, with a very profound bow, Harold Falcon left Mr McPul-

ham to conclude an operation which had been
delayed by so very unpleasant a communication.

McPulham took his breakfast in his own
room. Business of importance took him to
Ireland, and he trusted Carruthers would be able
to find a substitute for him as a rider.

Harold informed Dick of the result of his interview, and gave him a pithy account of its
details.

'And who was the other man who heard this
scheme of robbery concocted?'

'Upon my honour, Dick, I wish you could tell
me; that there was another besides me that heard
it all, is undoubted; and he's just as great a
scoundrel as the fellow who announces his intention of starting by the mail to-night for Ireland.
However, we're well rid of the most active con-
spirator, and you've nothing now to do but to
look after the horse. I'll do my part to win your
money, you may depend upon it.' Saying which
Harold turned short round, and walked off to the
stables, while Dick Carruthers admired the in-
genuity which had saved him a vast amount of
trouble, to say nothing of the prospect of a heavy
loss in pocket and reputation. Harold Falcon was
disposed to regard his successful deceit as an in-
genious device for saving his own.

In an hour or two they went to the races: it was the first day, and though the company usually reserved itself for the steeplechases, which was a sport then neither so common nor in so bad odour as since, there was a very handsome show of the county aristocracy, of the visitors, and of the racing community present. Amongst the first were conspicuous the occupants of Dick Carruthers' drag, which came on to the course with a form and character unapproachable in the present day, excepting by some half dozen of those noblemen and gentlemen who have brought with them an art learnt before the Stokers and Pokers were all-powerful. Charles Tyrwhitt Jones was then on the road, and Sir J. Vincent Cotton was on the Age. Sir Henry Peyton drove his piebalds, and John Spicer his grays. Lord Chesterfield, George Payne, Mr Villebois, Major Macgennis, the late Duke of Beaufort, and many more (whose mantles have descended on a chosen few, the present Duke, Captains Bastard and Cooper, Baillie, and Lord Poulett, and another Sir Henry Peyton), had brought to perfection one of the most beautiful of our national amusements. So on the course, among the well-appointed drags, and exactly opposite the grand stand, Harold Falcon drew up Dick Carruthers' team, a delight to the admiring crowd.

On the opposite side we have said was the grand stand. To those forming their notions of a stand from that of Ascot or Goodwood, of Epsom or Doncaster, it would have appeared homely; to the magnates of the county, to the manager, clerk, and handicapper, to the Town Council and the race-committee, the building in question was magnificent. Nothing seemed to be wanting. Having ascended the stairs, and paid your money, on the right was a private door leading to a room devoted to the stewards and their friends. From thence, through the open windows, they were enabled to address their acquaintances below, on the lawn, or to take the odds, which they were ever ready to do, offered in the modest tones of the ring-men, since then grown into a body, leviathan all over; leviathan in lungs, numbers, impudence, and estate.

Next to this was a longer stand, in which the beauty and elegance of the aristocracy and the visitors loved to sun itself. The gaping rustics from the course, and the betting-men, jockeys, gents, and linendrapers, stared with unabated curiosity at the silks, satins, ringlets, flowers, feathers and bonnets of the ladies; while they paraded themselves in light straps and badly fitting white-duck trowsers, cut-a-way coats, and four-and-ninepenny gossamers, futile imitations of the well-made clothes of their betters. But then you see we have known since then the happiness of an approaching equality; and the blessings of free-trade and the rights of man have enabled us all to dress pretty much alike: and all like blackguards. As, moreover, it was felt that there was a great distinction between the accredited swells of the county and any mere waifs and strays of Waterpark-life, this stand was barred to all but those who were prepared with a steward's ticket, price one guinea, instead of half that amount, and granted by voucher from the stewards, or master of the hounds.

The rest of the building was occupied by that mighty majority known as nobody, and by the payment of their half-guineas and crowns, adding mightily to the funds of the race-committee and to the respectability of the meeting. There was too a vast crowd of some thirty thousand vagabonds, who have since laid siege to Government for votes, and whom Mr Lowe recommends to pay a sufficient rental to get them. They enjoyed themselves very much, having arrived from a sort of black country in the neighbourhood, and taking pleasure in the racing as a make-shift for their favourite sport of cocking. The magistrates, driven by the legislature, or the legislature by the magistrates, had lately launched their thunderbolts against this; and as they couldn't make them learned, were determined to make them virtuous against their will.

In the first of these places, the stewards' seat, were the Duke of Chessingham, Admiral Target, Lord Chesshampton, Sir Samuel Corduroy, and a dozen others, with the master of the Waterpark hounds, and one of the members for the county. They were all gentlemen of good repute, honest, upright sportsmen; anxious for the integrity of the sport they professed to enjoy. The Duke of Chessingham had a great name, a vast estate, all of which he spent, and something more, having race-horses, and a pack of fox-hounds, a yacht, three large houses, and some extravagant sons. The Admiral was the very stay and backbone of racing, the terror of evildoers, the best handicapper in England, and one of the most unflinching denouncers of rascality wherever and whenever it came under his eye. As to Lord Chesshampton, his life was passed in the business of the turf. He had but four thousand a-year, and had five-and-forty horses in training. Lived upon it? of course he did; what in the world else was he to live on? He couldn't sweep the crossing at Limmer's— indeed that enviable *pied à terre* was occupied by a black man with a wooden leg, whose gains, however considerable, were dependent on regular work; while Lord Chesshampton's gains were said rather to depend upon regular play. But there they all were, and no man but a sceptic could doubt that their first object was the improvement of the breed of horses; an object which unfortunately up to this time they have never accomplished.

It was a very pleasant day; the racing was good, the people happy, and Mr Flimsey, the manager and clerk of the course, in his very best form. The glossy splendour of his toilet, the venerable roll of his hat, almost episcopal, the suavity of his manner, and the liberty of his conscience in favour of his friends' horses, left nothing to be desired. Everything was there, even to the dog, which occasionally appears on the course now, especially on Derby days. This year —Hermit's year—it was a black one.

Harold Falcon had won a hundred or two; but his mind had been singularly occupied in thinking of McPulham and his associate: who was he?

'What's become of McPulham, Dick?' inquired one or two, when they found him not on the coach.

'Business in Ireland. He's gone off to town to catch the night-mail to Holyhead.' It will be remembered that we are not writing of railroad days.

'Then he can't ride the Rover to-morrow. Who are you going to put up?'

'Harold Falcon's going to ride him.'

'He'll sell you, Dick—he's laid three thousand to one against him.'

'And taken seven. I think I can trust Harold if I can anybody.' And he certainly could. In the mean time Harold had a strong suspicion, but had no means of verifying it.

They were just leaving the course, when, in the crowd leaving the stand, Lord Cranstone and Harold were wedged together close to the Duke of Chessingham.

'Have you done any good to-day, Cranstone?' said the Duke.

'Lost like the devil, Duke. I've gone against the favourites, and they've done nothing but win all day.'

' So they will nine times out of ten, if they're really backed. The British public is a very good judge. Who rides Dick Carruthers' horse to-morrow ?'

' McPulham, I believe,' said Cranstone, with much coolness.

' I think not,' replied Harold. 'I have the mount.' He spoke loudly and pointedly, and watched the effect on Cranstone. It was electrical. Every particle of colour left his face for a minute, a stony look appeared in his large blue eyes, and then there returned his usual confident· smile, as he said, ' Nonsense, Falcon ; what's become of McPulham, then ? he was asked here on purpose to ride—he came with you this morning ?' And the same blank look took possession of him again, as he remembered that he had not seen him at all on the course. Lord Cranstone himself had ridden a hack up an hour before the time, as he wanted to get on something, and did not feel disposed to wait for the drag.

' No; he went to London this morning : and he's not likely to return.' By which time they were down-stairs. One went to the drag, the other to look for his hack, and the former knew who the partner in the conspiracy had been. But Falcon held his tongue, and watched him.

The fact is that his vigilance was thrown away. First of all, the honesty of Carruthers' servants was unimpeachable. Excepting by some manœuvre beyond Cranstone's unaided powers, the horse was quite safe. Beyond this, Cranstone's real opinion was that the horse could not win. He had laid against him long before; and, not satisfied with that, had backed Zitella. He had met with a ready tool or confederate by accident in Mr McPulham, and had endeavoured to make assurance doubly sure: his great fear was that he might have been detected. He saw no signs of that in the conduct of any of the party, and was persuaded that the Irishman was gone on some unexpected business, quite unconnected with the race.

Harold Falcon kept his suspicions to himself. As to Dick Carruthers, having got rid of the man who was likely to do him any injury, he was satisfied: and being perfectly comfortable in the hands of his friend Falcon, he gave himself no further anxiety on the subject.

CHAPTER XI.

THE RACE.

THE old-fashioned steeplechase of fifty years
ago was so totally different from those of modern
times, that I must devote a few lines to an explanation of the steps by which it had reached
its peculiar form at Waterpark, and which was
but a type of its present perfections.

There was a time, and men may regard it as
akin to the golden age, when a certain number
of enthusiastic foxhunters, having had a bad
day's sport, and having nothing to do with an
odd ten-pound note (which in the miserable slang
of these days would be called a 'tenner'), determined upon a pure trial of nerve and horseflesh
on their road home. A steeple is by no means
an unimportant object even in a hunting country; and the natural one to which a man's hopes
turn, metaphorically or literally, as a land-mark,
when no other is in view. The notion that any
particular compliment to the church was implied

is a mistake, due possibly to the ritualistic pro-
clivities of a Spurgeon or a Cumming, or some
other great man. Hence the word steeplechase,
which has remained in vogue long after the explanation of the most zealous respondent to
' Notes and Queries ' has died out, does not by
any means shadow forth the church as the object
of its pursuers.

The next step towards pure laicism was the
summary rejection of the steeple altogether; and
a start for any well-known point, as the flag on
the top of a hill, or the conservatory of a conspicuous gentleman's seat. Until in more degenerate times, finding that disputes arose as to
who first jumped on to the lawn or into the water-
butt, or who went up a lane or opened a gate,
and who did not, it was decided to mark out by
flags what might be considered a real course,
leaving the riders to go as close to, or as far
from, the line of demarcation, on the right or the
left, as they pleased : only stipulating that the
money would go to the gentleman who first
reached the goal.

It was admitted on all hands that the fun,
the money, and the honour was confined to the
riders, or nearly so ; and that if anybody came
to grief, nobody saw it. It was a happy time,

however, of exemption from gate-money and too
obtrusive swindling. It remained now for the
inhabitants of Waterpark to inaugurate a steeplechase, which should combine the dangers of a
natural country with the comforts of an artificial
spectacle. It was the very beginning of the cut-
and-dried Liverpool, Leamington, and Croydon
pattern; and which have themselves become
modifications of Market Harborough to suit the
capacity of the performers. I am a man of pro-
gress; I believe a two-year-old for five furlongs,
with six stone on its back, is the true step towards the improvement of the thorough-bred
horse for general purposes; I wear everything but
a beard, an all-round collar, and a wide-awake;
I believe in the British artisan; I adore a chig-
non when made of the lady's own hair and made
up at a first-rate purveyor's; but I do not believe
in the utility of the modern steeplechase course
to give quickness, nerve, or knowledge of country to our horsemen. When we once enclosed
in posts and rails the limits of the course, and
sat in judgment over the rotten banks of a brook,
and the too stiff timber of a double post and rails,
we reduced one-half or two-thirds the courage,
the quickness of observation, the judgment, and
the true intelligence of our jockeys. The pace is

different, the horse is different, and the man is different. The man who can ride fast enough and well enough sometimes to win on a beaten course, where he knows the fences and the ground, would have no chance over a country which he has never seen with the men who used to find their way over Leicestershire on Clasher and Clinker.

'How's the horse this morning, Stevens?' said Harold Falcon on the day of the race, wandering out after breakfast towards the box.

'Bright as a star, captain. Would you like to see him?' and the two went in and found him nibbling a handful of oats that had been thrown in to him.

The Rover was a large good-looking horse, thorough-bred; for which, by-the-way, he had to give an allowance of seven pounds to all the half-bred ones in the race—the onus of proving them thorough-bred lying with the opponent, if they were not in the stud-book. He was a dark chestnut, with one white leg behind. His head and neck were handsome and set on for pulling. Falcon said he gave you a nice feel of the former, some said he carried his rider in his mouth. His shoulders were thick, but well laid back, so as to give his quarters a great appearance of height

and length. His thighs were large, and his hocks
fine and clean, but very broad ; and he had plenty
of length. He did not look very good-tempered,
but, to say that he wanted a little riding, is all
that his worst enemies could allege to his disadvantage.

'At three o'clock that afternoon Harold Falcon took his gallop, preliminary to the steeplechase on the Waterpark course. He was the
beau-ideal of a gentleman-jockey; which name
I use in the absence of a better. His colours
were green, with gold belt and black cap; his
neck-cloth was white, his breeches were just
sufficiently roomy to give him ease in his seat,
and his long straight legs were clothed in tops as
white and closely fitting as if they had been made
upon the trees. A gentleman on a racecourse in
brown tops did not belong to the golden age of
steeplechasing.

' How do you like the look of him, Cranstone?'
said Lord Chesterton.

' I never liked his shoulders : look at the mare,
how well she moves ; he gives seven pounds to
her and the Emperor.' But though Lord Cranstone spoke cheerfully he had a very anxious look.

' And he's able to do it,' said Childers : ' look
at his shoulders; besides, he's a thorough-bred

one, and if they come to difficulties it's a guinea
to a shilling on the horse.'

'I can't agree with you; and as to his
shoulders, they're the very point I should com-
plain of.' But Lord Cranstone knew nothing of
shoulders until he sat upon them.

'Why, Carruthers, what's this—this thing in
black, coming now? I thought there were but
three going for it;' and Lord Cranstone leant
down from the drag to speak to his friend. He
was pale and nervous, but this new appearance
had a cheering effect upon him.

'Why, it's the horse they've just made a
favourite in the ring at three to one,' replied
Carruthers. I don't understand it.'

'Who's that on him—isn't it Oliver?' asked
the other.

'Yes. I understand it now; it's Pullaway, with
Tom Oliver on him. They said they couldn't run
him because P. wouldn't ride him. I see it all
now; they've put up Tom Oliver, and given the
seven pounds' allowance. He's not thorough-bred,
so he and my horse run at even weights.' Cranstone's excitement grew painful, as the chances in
his favour increased, and Dick Carruthers looked
proportionately sulky. The most perfectly un-
moved person of the lot was Harold Falcon.

They were walking up to take their places—
the race beginning and ending at the grand
stand. 'Here, Dick,' said Harold. 'I know
this horse has a little temper; I can feel it in him.
Have you any orders to give?'

'Yes; win my money for me, and don't kill
the horse.' And as this was an answer highly
characteristic of the owner, Harold determined
upon fulfilling it to the letter, if he could. In
another minute they were 'Off.'

Pullaway took the lead, Tom Oliver in his
black jacket was over the first fence—a stiff flight
of rails well in advance—sitting on his horse and
holding him as if in a vice. The other three came
on in a ruck, all of them getting safely over the
first fences without a mistake. The Emperor
appeared a little overpaced; and Zitella and the
Rover went on side by side, ten lengths behind
the black jacket. Harold was right about the
Rover. He soon found that he liked his own way,
which was to the front; but Pullaway continued
his lead at such a pace that Harold doubted
the policy of running up to him. He was right.
They had been going a mile, when, by delicate handling, the horse became more tractable;
and as Harold and he became better acquainted,
he ceased to fight, and laid himself out to gallop.

At the same time Pullaway began to come back to him, while Zitella was pulled back. They were now about a mile from the start, and nothing very formidable had yet presented itself in the way of fencing.

At this turn of the course they began to descend, and it was seen that they would be lost to the sight of the crowd on the stand, excepting to those quite on the top of it. By the number of people who had assembled at the next fence, it was evident to Harold that it was a rasper. Tom Oliver too was of the same opinion, as he took a pull at his horse, and allowed the Rover to come within a couple of lengths of him. Zitella and her rider were not equally impressed with so obvious an act of prudence, and shooting forward came heavily against a second rail : the advantages of pace were made manifest by the manner in which she divided the timber, landing into the plough without further accident than a severe stumble ; Emperor took advantage of the hole she had made for him ; and the Rover and Pullaway, better handled, jumped it handsomely, and went on with the running.

They were now out of the course, and their line for the next mile and a half was only marked by flags, which were to be kept on the left-hand

of each. Two consummate horsemen like Oliver
and Harold Falcon were not likely to select such
ground as the present for racing, and seeing the
nature of the next meadows, which were low and
marshy, they both rode with additional care.
The rider of Zitella, with a laudable anxiety to be
first some part of the race, took up the running;
and having the best of the weights, made his
way over the water-meadows down to the brook.
Here as usual a crowd had assembled, and but
that the more formidable piece of water was to be
jumped in sight of the stand, probably the population of Waterpark and its vicinity would have
been present to see the fun.

The first at it was Zitella, a little pumped, she
slipped round, and her example was ignominiously
followed by the Rover, while Pullaway and the
Emperor got safely over. In another minute
Harold was again on the same side as his opponent, but twenty lengths behind, while Zitella
had not joined them. The next field was sound
grass-land, ascending again into what might be
called the course, and about a mile and a half
from home. Here Harold made play, taking advantage of his horse's breeding; and upon coming
into the course over a bound fence with the ditch
from him, he was again within three lengths of

Pullaway. The Emperor was here disposed of, though he continued to fence well throughout. The pace was too good for him; and as they came on over the fences, without a mistake, the shouts of 'Pullaway' reached the ears of the riders from the stand.

And now the artificial brook was being neared at every stride; fourteen feet of water, but conveniently made with a low fence bent over it on the taking-off side. On they came, Tom Oliver still leading, who landed his horse handsomely, while three lengths behind him the Rover followed suit. Both were still hard held, neither of them yet riding. The intervening fences before the run-in were not difficult, and Pullaway, with perhaps the best horseman in England, certainly the strongest, on him, continued his lead. Harold felt his horse; he had still enough in him to run home, if Pullaway could do no more, and it might still be a neck and neck affair. Tom Oliver looked round somewhat confidently, when Harold, thinking his time was come, caught his horse by the head, and with a determination which astonished the Rover, began to run up to his opponent. The shouts increased, as now at his girths they came along the course, one single flight of hurdles alone remaining. Side by side they were jumped, and as they landed, there still remained the one half-length between them. Already they were opposite the stand, Pullaway with his head and shoulders still in front, when, within two lengths of the winning-post, by a rush that would have done credit to Chifney, Harold Falcon let his horse out, and amidst an excitement that had never been seen in Waterpark before, made a 'dead-heat' of the race of the meeting.

The scene that ensued lives in the memory of those who saw it. Of course both parties abused the judge, that understands itself, as the Germans say. The Rovers and the Pullaways both claimed the victory, and both appealed to the stewards. If those august persons do little for the honour that is thrust upon them, they at least serve to decide such a point as the present. The judge's fiat must be respected; and as neither party was satisfied, it only remained to run off the dead-heat at five o'clock the same afternoon.

Cranstone was flushed and excited, though reassured by the confident assertions that Tom Oliver could not lose on a beaten horse.

'Why didn't Harold come sooner?' said one.

'Tom Oliver was caught napping for once in his life,' said another.

Those who knew nothing of the mistake at the water wondered how he ever let Tom Oliver get away from him. Everybody knew better than the riders themselves.

The Duke of Chessingham thought he had never seen a finer bit of riding, but laid three to two pretty freely after the race against the Rover. Harold took it to a hundred without giving his reasons, which rather encouraged Dick Carruthers and his party. Sir Samuel Corduroy went to look at the horses, and fancied Pullaway had everything taken out of him to do what he had done; and, said he, 'I think the thorough-bred one will come soonest round.'

'Admiral Gorget thought they ought to divide, and—'

'How about bets?'

'Put them together, and divide—there's no difficulty about that.'

'They won't divide now,' said Lord Keswick: 'there's Falcon backing himself; and three to two has put them all on their mettle.'

The ladies were especially enthusiastic about Harold; and the duchess thought it would serve the duke right if he lost his money. As Harold walked out of the weighing-room, with a thick pea-jacket over his colours, he met with a perfect ovation from the crowd. Tom Oliver's face, too, looked a little anxious, though he said nothing. He thought it was no odds either way.

The other races passed off without comment. The people evidently were intent upon the coming contest. It was to come off in two hours, and there were three races to be decided before that time. Nobody looked at them with their usual anticipation of pleasure; they were but so many steps to the accomplishment of a much more interesting affair.

At last the Rover and Pullaway came out. You could scarcely have told that they had been out before. There was no preliminary canter, and they were started at once—both inclined to wait. At length Pullaway took the lead by a length, and went on with the running as before. This time there was no refusals, and the only thing to be remarked was that the pace was moderated. When they emerged from the heavy lands once more into sight, they were both being ridden well and judiciously—neither meant to throw a chance away. About a mile from home they began to increase the pace; at the brook they were side by side, and both got over cleverly, Pullaway dropping his hind legs a little, when two-thirds of the course were passed. Cranstone wrote a short note, which he sent over to the drag to apologize for going unexpectedly to town. Before it reached its destination Harold Falcon had won a good race by a length—cleverly.

CHAPTER XII.

HOW TO PAY A DEBT OF HONOUR WITHOUT MONEY.

THERE could be no doubt that when Harold Falcon woke the next morning, notwithstanding his natural and acquired indifference to impecuniosity, he was much more comfortable in his mind than he had been lately. When a man is really living from hand to mouth, with the exception of some bare pittance, a windfall of four thousand pounds is worth a consideration; and is apt to brighten the horizon of futurity, at least for a time to come. It was so with Harold. Not that he regarded it as possibly many of my readers might have done. To a man reared as a gentleman, who really sees himself within one hundred pounds of the workhouse; who knows that another month must take him out of his comfortable home into a sponging-house or a debtor's prison; that he has on a coat, waistcoat, and trowsers which are to last for ever, or until they be exchanged for a shroud; that has no

hope in race-horses, or relatives—such a windfall
as four thousand pounds sounds like eternal water
in the desert to the dying traveller, the pool of
Siloam to the incurable leper. It must not be
supposed that this was the case with Harold
Falcon. He didn't even look at its prospective
advantages, as an end, but only as a means for
accomplishing still greater ends. If my friends
and publishers, Messrs ——, were to offer me
such unheard-of remuneration for this or any
future efforts—and no man can say what they may
do—I should think it my duty to purchase some
railway debentures, limited liability discount part-
nership, monster hotel shares, or other permanent
and secure investment. Such was not Harold's
view of the matter at all. He lay in bed thinking
only how he might most profitably invest a certain
portion in the coming Derby, and wondering
whether the hints about Mr Rawlinson's horse
and Lord Chesterfield's mare were to be relied
on. He gave a thought to old Jansen, determin-
ing that the old money-lender should have his
score cleared off as soon as possible; and rejoiced
in thinking that he had done with him, at all
events till the next time. Harold knew what it
was to win money, occasionally, and more frequently to lose it; but four thousand pounds

was a haul, which he had not effected lately.

It was the second day after the steeplechase; and Falcon was still at the Holt. He came downstairs with more even than his usual goodhumour. On his way down he met with Dick Carruthers, who asked him when he wanted to go. 'I suppose you can stay a day or two longer.'

'Yes: I've nothing to do till settling day— let's see, this is Friday.'

'Yes. What do you win altogether?'

'A hundred or two on the Tuesday, a thousand from Spielman, and the difference between seven and four thousand on the steeplechase: the odds I laid you.'

'I'm glad of it. It served Cranstone right. I don't know what he lost, but he had two bad days I'm sure. He never would believe the horse could gallop.'

'I'm sorry for Cranstone myself,' replied Harold. 'He's had the worst luck consecutively I've ever heard of on the turf. I'd rather have won my seven thousand of any other man of my acquaintance. It will cost him ten to get it.'

'I hope he will get it, for your sake, Falcon.'

'So do I, for yours.' Saying which with a careless laugh they walked into the breakfastroom.

They found the greater number of those who had been spending the week at the Holt already at the table. They were reading the papers of the day before, and the letters which had just come over from Waterpark. 'Any news, Borodaile?' inquired Dick Carruthers.

'Yes. Mr Hall, the sitting magistrate at Bow-street, has locked up a certain Mr Johnson for thrashing a policeman, and offers it as his opinion that he is a marquis of sporting celebrity much too fond of disturbing the peace of the Haymarket. He declines accepting a fine. Pleasant for Johnson.

'Very—he'll get rid of his connection with the aristocracy as quickly as possible, I should think. But the Haymarket must be a good deal altered if there's any peace in it to disturb,' said Childers.

'Who is Johnson, I wonder,' said Carruthers.

'A quiet man in the fifteenth, who happens to be very like W—d, and has only been in two rows in his life. They fined him very heavily once before for his unfortunate resemblance.'

'Here's a man been shot in a duel; and the principal and seconds are gone to Boulogne.'

'Who is he?' inquired Sir Harry Trenchard.

'It doesn't say. The man who shot him was a linendraper's apprentice.'

'It's about time gentlemen gave up killing one another then,' said Lord Chesterton, who opened the door just as the passage was read from the newspaper.

'Or themselves,' said Lord Borodaile, who suddenly dropped the paper into his plate, and fell back in his chair. 'Good God, how horrible! Poor Cranstone.'

The man next to Lord Borodaile picked up the paper, and happening to be less intimately acquainted with him than the former, was able to read a short paragraph from the *Times,* while the rest of Dick Carruthers' guests heard him with the most painful astonishment.

The paper announced that Lord Cranstone had posted up to town on Wednesday evening from Waterpark—that he had gone to bed as was supposed upon reaching his house in Mayfair; and that on his non-appearance the following day, his valet had broken open his bed-room door. Lord Cranstone was found sitting in his arm-chair quite dead, and a phial which was still in his hand left no doubt that he had destroyed himself with prussic acid. His betting-book was open by his side, and his undoubted losses were the clue to the motive for the rash act.

This was the substance of the *Times'* report,

and there were at least three or four present who had no reason to doubt its correctness.

Harold Falcon was a man of considerable self-possession; but it would have required a stoic indeed to have seen his newly-formed hopes dashed to the ground without a pang. He changed colour, but never made a remark, and not a soul looked at him, though some there must have guessed his feelings. In the general exclamations, queries, regrets, doubts (for some were expressed), and surmises, Harold Falcon got up and left the room. It was a curious fact that, notwithstanding his own ruin, for it really was so comparatively, he smiled to himself at the chance remark he had made to Dick Carruthers. As to that worthy, he was quite acute enough to know that his money would be forthcoming somehow or other, and much too selfish to dream of offering accommodation, which he guessed must be taken.

Harold retired to his own room. He sat down and wiped his brow, on which a cold perspiration had broken out. Then he looked in the glass, and was surprised to see that his face had recovered neither its wonted colour nor serenity. His hands and limbs trembled, at present, and he poured some cold water into his basin and held his hands and face in it for a few minutes. After a time he began to realize the facts of his position. He was no better off than before, and he owed his friend Dick Carruthers four thousand pounds into the bargain. He had no means of getting it; and he had a very great reluctance to be in Dick's debt. He was one of those sanguine persons who never hesitated to run the risk of repaying five hundred with about sixty per cent., out of an income of two or three hundred a-year and contingencies; but he shrank from the responsibility of thousands. It really was a heavy obligation for a dependent and very extravagant ex-guardsman.

Presently he rang the bell.

'Send my servant here, and ask Mr Carruthers to allow me the use of a hack this morning.' And Mr Carruthers' man hurried off.

'Now, Pearson, pack my things up, and go into Waterpark this afternoon. Be at the 'Regent' at four o'clock, and take two places by the mail. We shall be in London late, but I can dine at the club, while you get my rooms ready.'

And Pearson, as invaluable as all poor men's servants are, whether from the hope of better times, or that they are urged by a sort of compassion to happier exertions, set about his task at once.

'Mind that cap and the jacket,'—and it is

rather remarkable that, while he felt fully impressed with the idea that they would not be wanted again, he was the more particular in his directions about them :—' and just run down and ask Stevens whether they can have a hack for me in a quarter of an hour. If the boy can be at the " Regent" at a quarter before four he shall bring it back, as I shall not return here.'

From Waterpark to Woodstock is a beautiful ride. A great part of it lies through fine park-like land, covered with magnificent timber, and presenting much variety of country. When Harold started, the first object was to reach Jansen's house in good time ; but as the sun got up, and the light became more dazzling, he pulled his horse into a walk and let him move slowly through the shadow of the trees, which were just beginning to put forth their leaves. To admirers of physical beauty Harold Falcon thus presented a rare picture.

He was of more than middle height, thin, active, straight, but broad and flat in the shoulders, and showing limbs of much elegance and symmetry. He had dark hair and dark eyes, a straight line of soft wavy whisker, which shaded a rather pale oval cheek. His nose and mouth were sufficiently handsome, and the latter especially was

adorned with a very fine set of teeth. His hair,
which on either side appeared from beneath his
hat, was dark and wavy.   His dress was perfectly consonant with the fashion of the day.   A
loose riding coat with broad skirts and metal
buttons, of a dark-green mixture, and bound with
a black silk braid or binding; a pair of buckskin
trowsers, fastened below his well-polished Wellington boots, completed the riding costume of a
gentleman of the year 184—.   He sat, when at a
foot-pace, well back on his horse; and his reins,
which were held in each hand nearly as far back as
his hips, gave every liberty to his horse's head, as
he walked along at four good miles in the hour.

His thoughts were sombre enough.   To say
they were not of himself and his own fortunes
would not be true.   No man faces poverty as he
was doing without much pain, much anxiety; but
while he thought of himself, he recurred frequently to the terrible fate of Lord Cranstone.   It
seems selfish enough to console yourself by the
superior misery of your fellow-creatures, or to
contrast favourably your own ills with their
heavier misfortunes.   But it gives a hopeful tone
to a mind depressed to think others have borne,
with patience and success, more than we.   Yes,
with patience—but where was Cranstone now?

How long Harold had known him, all smiles, carelessness, indifference! the boon companion, never without money to throw away, never with enough to pay his debts: Where was he now? and who could guarantee him against a like fate? The tears almost came to his eyes as he looked back at what he had been, and forward to what he might be. If he had but money—but for money he never had had a care in his life. How many can echo Harold's sentiment! God only knows how many he might have had with it.

Lord Cranstone came of age a comparatively rich man. No pleasure was too extravagant, no luxury inaccessible. He lived in an age of bold rivalry; and the only means of competition was by gambling. He dissipated every shilling at Crockford's and on the turf. The Jews were tired at length of a doubtful sixty per cent., preferring a positive forty; unable to procure it, and indebted to his friends, who would have saved him, bad as he was, at four times the money, he destroyed himself. This he called honour—amongst other of honour's attributes, it's very short-sighted.

CHAPTER XIII.

WHERE HAROLD GOT THE MONEY TO PAY HIS DEBTS
OF HONOUR.

BERNHARD JANSEN was a man of peculiar manners as well as appearance, as the reader already knows. His displeasure with his wife and daughter, richly as it was merited, was not consistent, or firm, or judicious in any way. It was capricious, violent at times, and gloomy ; and as apt to bestow itself upon the man's inner self as upon the offending persons.

When Harold Falcon presented himself at the house, Jansen was brooding gloomily over the disgrace, which his instinct told him would fall sooner or later upon his name. Had Harold had to select a time for his business, he would not have chosen this above all others, but he had no choice ; time was pressing, and his name wanted saving as well as Jansen's.

Having given his hack to a boy in the old

stable-yard, and bid him put a cloth over his loins, which he did by use of a couple of meal sacks, he walked unannounced into the presence of Mrs Jansen. That lady was wholly unprepared for the visit, as might have been seen by her dress and occupation. She was assisting her domestic servant in the preparation of Herr Jansen's dinner, with her sleeves tucked up above the elbows, to give the freer use to her arm in wielding a rolling pin. A large apron, which came over her shoulders and chest, and descended to her feet, covered a dilapidated black silk dress.

Harold saw that he had made a mistake in his route, and drew back at the door. 'Mr Jansen I was looking for—finding no servant and—'

Mrs Jansen's sleeves were already down ; but all her usual alacrity was gone. She was meek, humble, depressed, for this once, and only said,

'Captain Falcon, Mr Jansen is in his room :' and thither he followed. For the first time in his life he saw traces of tears on the lady's face.

Jansen was hard at work—he had before him a fine piece of carving in design from part of the cathedral at Seville. He was attempting to copy its most difficult and remarkable details. Excessive difficulties soothe, if they do not calm, mental agitation. Jansen found it so now. He had had

a violent paroxysm that day; he had converted
it into gloom.

'Hallo, Jansen,' said Harold, ushered into
the room by the wife, who however shut the door
on him at once. 'Hard at work;' and then he
took up a piece of very handsome carving, and
began to expatiate on its beauties. For Harold
could take high art of various kinds, and was not
utterly ignorant of it. Many men were not
ashamed of refinement thirty years ago; and it
put Jansen usually in good humour. It wanted
something more than high art now.

It was quite clear that Harold could not
plunge at once into his necessities, which are not
like a pair of good trowsers, but must be handled
gently and tenderly, as having had many a patch,
and in places utterly threadbare; amenable to
the heel of a boot, or highly susceptible of tight
straps and unprepared movements.

'That's a beautiful piece of work, Jansen,
you're employed on now.' The artist looked up,
but didn't reply. 'Your countrymen excel in it.'

'Do you think so, Captain Falcon? Gibbons
was an Englishman. He did much in Chats-
worth and Windsor. I knew nothing finer than
the room at Petworth.'

'Gibbons was of Dutch extraction, Jansen,

like yourself. Have you seen the foliage and flowers in the Chapel of Trinity, Oxford?' The mention rather jarred upon the old man, and he replied,

'I never go out. I've scarcely crossed the garden five times in the last ten years; and don't care if I never do again.'

'It's worth seeing, nevertheless,' said Harold, quite ignorant of the cause of his ill-humour.

'But you didn't come here to tell me that. If it's money, I don't see how I can help you.' And here Herr Jansen began again at his work.

'You've never failed me yet, Jansen; but this is a heavier business. Somebody must help me, or I'm ruined.' And the tone of Harold's voice sounded so sadly and despondingly as he pronounced the last word, that Jansen looked up at him, and was surprised to see how unlike himself the Captain was.

'Ruined! I've never seen one of you gentlemen that wasn't ruined at one time or another. You never come here till you are. There are plenty would like to be ruined in the same way. Shall I tell you what ruin means, Captain Falcon?—three months' inconvenience, perhaps a renewal, a year or two in Paris or the north of Italy, and then the repentant prodigal, or the long-expected legacy.   Isn't it so ?'   And Jansen continued his work.

'Not with me.   Did you ever hear of Lord Cranstone ?'

'And of his death.   He owes me a couple of hundred.'

'And me—seven thousand.   It's all I had.' The old workman looked up.

'And now you're a beggar do you say?   You're only where you were before?'

'Worse ; I laid off four thousand of it,' replied Harold Falcon.

'And how much do you want ?   Won't your creditor wait ?'

'I don't intend to ask him.'

'You must.'

'I'd rather follow Cranstone's example !'   And perhaps for the moment so bitter was Harold's feeling of debasement that he half meant what he said.

'No, you mustn't do that.   Go abroad.'

'What, run away ? that's as bad.   Will you clear my book at Tattersall's, and give me a thousand to go with ?'   And Harold spoke with a mocking tone, as if the thing was quite out of the question.

'What security have you to offer?'

'Nothing—not even a father's death to speculate upon. There's a good old lady, Mrs Falcon, my father's aunt, who might leave me twenty thousand—who will do so when she dies.'

'Nobody lends thousands on old women's fancies. They're very capricious.'

'Well, I've nothing else, Jansen, I've told you, but my allowance; at present it pays my cabs and my tailor. Henceforth, I must live on it.'

'Can't you get me a joint name, a good name.'

'What! for four thousand or thereabouts—par exemple, very likely. Besides, why should I rob my friend?'

'Drowning men catch at straws.'

'Right enough, but then they do the straws no mischief.'

'Do you see no plank?'

'None that would save me; plenty that I could swamp, if they would swim with me.'

'Would you insure your life for four thousand, Captain Falcon?'

'You're afraid of me, then?'

'No, I'm not afraid of you; but would you do it?'

'I would, and pay the premium as long as I could.'

'And what would you do with four thousand pounds?'

'I'd pay up on Monday, and go abroad with the remainder. But I don't see what that matters to you unless you mean to lend it.'

'You would go abroad?'

'I would do anything to escape from this position. Will you help me? As I am in your debt, I am bound to listen to your advice, even if I do not take it.' For with all his careless good-humour, Harold had reached a point whence he could see nothing but misery. Anything but application to his uncle, who had already done so much for them.

Jansen hesitated a moment, and then, weighing his words well, said,

'You would do anything? marriage?'

'For money? be it so : a wrinkled old woman, or a hideous young one?'

'Neither. A few thousands, it is true ; beauty wonderful, youth, accomplishments. Your family (have you one ? I think not,) objects. Go from the church-door abroad ; and when the good old aunt is gone, the world will worship you and your wife, as long as the twenty thousand lasts.'

In all his disappointment, Harold Falcon could not help laughing at this curious proposal so quaintly made. So he said in reply, 'and who's the lady?'

'Come and let us look for her,' said Jansen. And as the giant rose from his seat with a grave and mysterious look, Harold Falcon felt himself compelled to follow this Dutch Mephistopheles; which he did with a mind more ill at ease than ever.

A quarter of an hour or thereabouts had elapsed, when Harold Falcon opened the door of the farm-house and passed out. He was followed by Bernhard Jansen. Neither spoke, and the former strode on towards the stables. He was deadly pale; his features worked with suppressed emotions, the most marked of which was the determination which kept the whole in subjection. His hat was drawn closely over his eyes; and in passing the windows of the house he kept them firmly fixed upon the ground. The boy who had before thrown the sacks over his horse's loins led him out, and having brushed out the wisps of hay which clung to his mane held the stirrup for the Captain to mount.

'You'll not forget the arrangement, Captain Falcon?' said Jansen, speaking for the first time, and with more respect in his manner than usual.

'The bargain, you mean, Jansen; call it by

its right name;' with which unpromising speech
Harold rode slowly out of the yard, and across
the pleasaunce, or dismantled park, in which the
artist's house stood.

It was not the road, nor even quite the direction, in which he wished to go ; but his horse
took the grass by preference (a very unusual
thing with horses) and wandered on, the reins
lying idly on his neck, and the rider's thoughts
travelling anywhere but on his way.

He crossed the park diagonally, and so absorbed was Harold in his own thoughts, that,
until his horse stood still at a stone wall in the
corner, by which there was no egress, he had not
discovered his mistake. Being thus brought up
by a regular Oxfordshire wall, of at least four
feet high, his first impression was bewilderment
as to how he got there ; the second a perception
that he could not reach his destination without
getting out or going round. At any other time,
fine horseman though he was, he would certainly
have preferred the latter course, as he was not a
man to risk his own neck or his friend's hack by
hazardous larking. On the contrary now : having
collected himself sufficiently to perceive that the
road to Waterpark would be hit by a cross-coun-
try ride to the right, and not feeling by any

means disposed to return by the yard through which he had come, he drew back his horse about forty or fifty yards, and gathered him together with a light hand but determined grip. He rode him slowly at the wall, the first thirty yards at a trot from which he broke into a slow canter; but the hack refused, and turned away to the right. As the wall was too high to jump at a stand he was obliged to let him come round. Then he compressed his lips, and the second attempt was successful. Increasing his pace a little, and bringing his horse so steadily up to it as to give him no room to turn, he found himself obliged to jump, and the two landed safely on the other side. Then Harold's blood began to stir within him, and crossing the next pasture and jumping the fence, holding his horse in a fair hand-gallop from field to field, and getting safely over the obstacles as they presented themselves, he struck the road to Waterpark over a stiffly-bound fence with the ditch beyond, in his stride. As he landed safely and pulled up, his colour had returned, and he patted the hack approvingly. His gloom was partly gone, and his mind made up for action. 'I made my bed; I must lie on it. It's a hard one, but it might have been worse, or such as Cranstone's. I'll not turn back now. Besides,

it's the only loophole. Come up.' Such was
the effect of his ride.

At a quarter before four he rode into Waterpark, and alighting at the 'Regent,' he threw his
rein to the boy who had been sent from the Holt
for the hack, and sauntered into the hotel.

'The coach would be through in ten minutes'
time,' said the landlady, 'and she knew Captain
Falcon's servant had booked two places. Captain
Falcon was not looking well; would he take anything ?' Captain Falcon ordered a pint of sherry
and sat down in the coffee-room.

'Waiter.' The waiter said, 'yessir,' all in
one word, as waiters will, and continued giving
change to another waiter at the farther end of the
room. Having finished his own business, he
slipped a napkin under his arm and asked Harold
what he pleased to want.

'Is the mail always punctual ?'

'Very, sir, very. Leastways I bin here five-
and-twenty year, and I never knowed it late but
once, that was in a snowdrift.'

Having re-assured himself he rose from his
table, and paced the coffee-room ; every two or
three minutes he looked out of the window.

His impatience was remarkable, and the delay

intolerable. But the coach was pretty punctual notwithstanding; and having taken only two minutes and a half to change horses, and put Harold's luggage into the boot, he got up in front and his servant behind, and they started for London with fifty miles to be done by nine o'clock. With the team they drove there was not much doubt about their doing it.

When Harold Falcon had made himself comfortable he turned suddenly round and encountered the face of an acquaintance, nothing more. He had met him at Oxford once or twice, and lately dined with him at the Holt. It was Beauchamp.

They exchanged greetings, and began a promising conversation, which developed itself by degrees from the weather, racing, bribery, Macadam, field-preaching, and such general topics to something domestic or social.

'Have you seen my cousin George, lately?' inquired Falcon.

'No, I haven't,' said the other with a very startled and puzzled look, a look which seemed to say, 'that's a very curious question to have asked.' 'No, I haven't.'

'Do you know where he is?' said the other very innocently, but looking equally astonished

at his neighbour; and wondering why he should
hesitate, as he appeared to do, to answer a simple
question.

'Where he is?' repeated Beauchamp, as if
pausing and weighing the words before he returned answer, 'what, don't you know—'

'Of course I don't,' replied Falcon, who was
somewhat impatient at getting no direct answer.
'Of course I don't—that's why I asked you.'

'Don't you know what they say? I was going
to ask you.'

'I can't say that I do; but if you'll tell me I
shall be much obliged.'

'Well, they do say—mind I don't myself
know that it is so; but they do say that he's gone
off with Jansen's daughter, and that your uncle
is furious, as of course he naturally would be.'

'I know that he isn't gone off with Jansen's
daughter, and of course my uncle is not so furious
as he might be. Just give me a light—thanks.'
And from that time, till they reached London,
when it was dark and cold, Falcon did not say
much more.

CHAPTER XIV.

HAROLD'S OTHER COUSIN.

OF course in those days there was no such thing as a Saturday half-holiday. It would naturally have been asked for what clerks and apprentices were meant. The notion of saving a material which did not really belong to the employer, which, like all machinery, was meant to be worn out, and which in the increase of population was sure to be renewed, never entered the philanthropist's head. The consequence of this was that there was no difficulty in transacting business on the last day of the week any more than on the first, among the Jews.

In pursuance, therefore, of his plans, Harold Falcon walked down St James's-street, and crossing over Pall-mall next door to what was afterwards the Guard's Club, walked into Hammersley's, and presented a cheque.

It was for a large amount, and the clerk to

whom it was presented, after a few minutes' absence and consultation with the senior of his department, disappeared into a room at the back of the bank.

'Would you be good enough to look at that,' said the man to the junior partner, who was sitting at a desk, running through figures with a most alarming alacrity. This extreme facility was a remarkable gift of one gentleman in that calling, and had acquired for him the name of Three-fingered Jack, from the manner in which at one time he allowed his fingers to run down the three columns of pounds, shillings, and pence, invariably finishing with a correct calculation.

'It's a large sum,' said the man in authority, looking up from his own calculations, and taking the document in his hand. 'Who presents it?'

'Captain Falcon, I believe, sir, himself.'

'What, the Captain Falcon of the Guards. Lord Falconberg's nephew?'

'I think it is, sir.'

'Ask him to do me the favour to walk in,' and Harold entered.

'Captain Falcon, will you take a chair for one moment,' which he did, and the junior partner rapidly finished his column and turned round.

'You want this money immediately—to-day?' inquired the banker.

'Immediately, if possible,' replied Harold.

'Will you forgive an impertinence from an old acquaintance of your uncle. Do you know the drawer of this cheque?'

'I do: and am much indebted to him.'

'Be less so, as soon as you can. We have not so much in our hands of his by a few hundreds, but may receive notice by the evening post, if not, on Monday.' Harold looked a little blank at this intelligence. 'However, if you really want it this morning, we will cash this cheque on your own undertaking.' The man who spoke was a very handsome man, with large flashing dark eyes, a look of great and fearless honesty, and massive but fine features. He looked like a man in whom any one might confide. Harold felt half-inclined to do so, but recollected himself and said, 'I want to go abroad to-morrow, for some time, and I will give any necessary security that I can,' very much wondering what that might be.

'Then sign that, if you please. Mr Johnson, be good enough to cash that cheque for Captain Falcon.'

He did so, and Harold Falcon left Pall-mall with a heavier pocket and lighter heart.

It was mid-day, and the streets were not full. A few late treasury and foreign-office clerks were on their way down Bond-street to their offices, having scarcely rid their eyes of the dust and champagne of Willis's rooms, or the then fashionable amusements of driving hackney coaches or wrenching off door-knockers. At present, however, it was early in the season, and full swing was not yet given to these entertainments. Vauxhall was not yet open, and the happy attractions of monster balloons, which swelled the attendance at that arrack-smelling, oil-bespattered tea-garden, had to come. It was not till later in the season that twenty thousand people assembled to see a man go up accompanied by his parachute, to descend through two miles of atmosphere on his head, or to witness the pyrotechnic displays which set the gardens on fire and very nearly involved the Thames itself in the conflagration. So as Harold made his way up Bond-street, he did not meet so many of his friends as he might have done later in the day. Those whom he did meet were full of one subject; and that was their own.

'Hallo, Falcon,' said Marcus Crane, who was pulled up by a butcher's cart as he attempted to

cross Bruton-street, and which a free and en-
lightened British public allows to scatter its mud
and its murders at the rate of sixteen miles an
hour,—'how are you. Isn't this an awful business?'

'Awful!' said Harold, who had but one subject
of meditation.

'Why, if Lord John brings in this bill (they
talk of only an eight pound franchise), we are
utterly swamped in the counties; and some day
or other, you mark my words, every fellow will
be able to read and write, and labourers' wages
will be at fourteen shillings a-week!'

'Good-bye,' said Harold hurrying on.

'I say, Harold, this is a precious affair, isn't
it?'—this address came from a brother-officer,
Charley Greystoke, who, having an interest in the
turf, must have heard of Cranstone's death. 'The
Duke is out of his mind.'

'What! his uncle—you don't say so?'

'Egad! I do though. He talks of a competition examination for the army—and there's my
young brother Reginald has been at Harrow this
seven years. Never been anywhere else. How
the d—l is he to know how to write and spell
and all that sort of thing, you know?'

This was something like a complaint; but

Harold had the bad taste to wring his friend's hand and pass on. Between that corner and Grosvenor-square he met three or four more. Two congratulated him on his success with the Rover. One was in love with a new woman who had appeared in a velvet habit and on a chestnut horse somewhere, and who proved to be Caroline; and a fourth offered him some members' tickets for the Zoological Gardens for 'to-morrow. I was there last Sunday and there was nobody in town.' Harold declined them rather bitterly and walked on.

He knocked at a door of a house in Grosvenor-square.

'Is Lord Hawkestone at home?'

The man hesitated.

'Yes, sir, he is at home; but not very well. I dare say he will see you, sir, though he was not to be disturbed.'

'Then ask his lordship's man, Wrench; and if not I'll call again in the afternoon.'

'His lordship will see you, sir,' says Mr Wrench, coming down-stairs. 'The family is not in town, and my lord was breakfasting in his own room. Would you walk up, sir,' and Harold ascended to the first floor and knocked at the door of the room at the back.

'Harold, I'm delighted to see you;' and Lord Hawkestone welcomed his cousin very warmly.

'Your man seems to have more discretion than most people, Hawkestone. He told me you were not very well, but would perhaps see me.'

'Then I have to be grateful to him for speaking the truth—and now I do see you, you don't look well. What's the matter, Harold?'

'I might ask the same of you, if I were disposed to be curious,' said the other.

'Not much amiss. I caught cold on guard, and to tell you the truth I was rather upset by poor Cranstone's death. You know we were at Eton together, and though I had no great sympathy for his pursuits, still you can't see a fine fellow, one of the best of the order ten years ago, wrecked body and mind at his time of life without some regret;' and as Lord Hawkestone spoke, his handsome light blue eyes and open honest face showed how good and sincere was his nature. There was a character and intelligence in his features so noble, so spiritual, that he never lost by comparison with his cousin Harold in physical beauty; although the latter attracted more by the lightness of his spirit, and the *insouciant* carelessness of his disposition.

They then talked about ordinary matters connected with Lord Cranstone's death, and the circumstances which led to it. Lord Hawkestone spoke seriously enough on the subject; he was not a man to regard such a lesson lightly; and he knew well the growing spirit of gambling which clogged the best energies of many a man of his acquaintance, and which was wrecking noble hopes and aspirations for many an one. His own regiment was not free from the taint, as he knew; and he had striven to check it among the youngsters. He mourned silently over Harold's defection. He was certainly ignorant of the extent to which he had gone; but it was impossible to live in town on such intimate terms with him, even since he had left the army, without knowing how reckless and debased in his real nature he had become. He was the more alive to it because he loved Harold; he knew his father's liking for him, though he was not demonstrative; and he half suspected a tenderer feeling on the part of his sister Lady Helen. He was old enough to exercise some influence over him too; but not so much older than he as to take him to task, or to interfere in the arrangement of his affairs.

Again, though his nature and his heart had hardened and degenerated by that constant friction with absence of high and honourable motives, and by association with idle selfishness and self-gratification, Harold was still essentially a gentleman. No one could take a liberty with him. He was as honourable on the race-course as in the drawing-room. With all his debts and responsibilities, he had never been known to fail in his obligations; and money-lenders and bill-discounters, who are not unlike the devil in one thing, that they are not even as bad as they are painted, not only praised the captain, but were generally willing to accommodate him within reasonable limits. His present necessities were out of all reasonable limits, and but for the ready and mysterious aid afforded by the ex-professional Jansen, he could no longer have shown amongst his equals, and must have lived henceforth exiled and proscribed. And all because Cranstone has paid his debts of honour with prussic acid.

Now he was going to pay his debts, and then he would go into exile.

'Fred, I'm come to ask you to do me a favour.'

'I will if I can. Is it to give you room here? My father and Helen don't come up till the week after next. We shall have the house to ourselves.'

'No, no; nothing so pleasant;' and Harold

looked serious. 'Are you likely to go to Tatter-sall's on Monday?'

'Certainly not, Harold,' and Lord Hawkestone laughed at the notion quietly; 'but if you want me to do so for you I will.'

'I came to you, Fred, because I cannot trust any one so well as you to do the commission without talking about it; and you'll laugh, perhaps, but I am especially anxious that your father should not know it. If he must know my last escapade I should prefer it to come from you. I should have some mercy dealt out to me; at least by you and Helen.'

'Harold, are you sure you know your best friends, even in your scrapes? but come, what is it—what can I do?'

'Will you take charge of that,'—here Harold counted out just four thousand pounds,—'and pay it over to Captain Childers for Dick Carruthers? He's not coming himself, and Childers settles the half-dozen bets he has.'

'Do you mean, Harold, that you lost four thousand to Carruthers?'

'I am afraid I did.'

'And am I not to receive anything for you?'

'Nothing!' and as Harold Falcon thought of the cause he looked down.

'This must have caused you great inconvenience, Harold, or will do so. Why didn't you
come to me, old fellow ? '

'You couldn't have helped me, Fred ! and I
cannot trespass on you any further than I do
now.'

'Are we not cousins, Harold ? '

'We might be brothers, for all your father
has done for us.'

'I wish we were, Harold. Wasn't poor Cranstone one of your party at the Holt ? '

'He was.'

'They say he lost twelve thousand at the
Waterpark meeting ; seven on the steeplechase.
Is it true ? and if so, Harold, to whom ? '

Harold was silent for a second, and said,
'To me, Fred. When I heard of the business I
knew it must be true, and I felt as if I'd the poor
fellow's blood upon my head. If he only had
known how willingly I would have cancelled it.
But, Hawkestone, take the money, that's a good
fellow. Do me the last favour you can, for I
leave England to-morrow. I'm not given to
much sentiment, as you know ; but this thing,
what with the loss and what with its result, has
been too much for me.'

Then Lord Hawkestone took the money, and

put it in his pocket-book; and then he stood up in front of his cousin Harold (he was rather the taller of the two) and took both of his hands in his. The contrast was very extraordinary, but very beautiful. Harold was dark and younger looking, and now appeared sad and humbled; not looking his cousin in the face. Hawkestone was fair, and bright, and open, but with a severe and earnest expression.

'I'm glad you came to me, Harold. I'll do your bidding, and you shall go abroad to-morrow, if you will. Now look at me, old fellow. If my father hears of this he will be grieved. He has been a kind friend to you, Harold, and will be again. Is there no return you can make him— nothing you can do for him and for us. Give up this life. You have left the Guards; I'm sorry for it. The service lost a good officer. But let us see if we cannot do something. The Ministry owe us no little; and though we are slow at claiming it, they would scarcely resist the claim when made. I know if I have your word I shall be safe.'

'You have my word, Fred. When you see me again it shall not be as a professional gambler. I'll see what can be done. At present I'm going away; and by the time I return,' and Harold could not help smiling at his prophetic humour, 'you'll see that the turf will not be fit for a gentleman, and that he'd better be under than on it.'

'You're right, Harold. As a pleasure it has been the pursuit of gentlemen in mind and heart. There were plenty such when my father was young; and the names associated with it show it abundantly: but it was never their occupation. When a man begins to live by the turf he must resort to the measures of those who live with him. He must run false trials, stop horses, get them and keep them in the betting, for unworthy motives; he must suborn touts, trainers, jockeys; he must endeavour to delude everybody, and will end by deluding himself; and thirty years hence he will do so. God bless you, Harold. Let's know where to direct to; and when I can help you, don't think of me as a cousin but as a friend.'

Harold walked down-stairs, and his hat was low down on his eyes when he passed out into the street.

CHAPTER XV.

ECONOMY.

FRAU JANSEN had done with intriguing; and Peggy Jansen, who was home again, submitted in a half-sulky, half-frightened silence to the dictates of her father. In other words, she was confined to her room, where the poor girl wept in silence, and prayed for some deliverance from the capricious humours of an injudicious scold and the furious violence of an obstinate madman. It is not too much to say that Bernhard Jansen was really, or chose to appear, partially and fitfully insane.

It had never been impossible hitherto to evade these fits of ill-temper or violence by avoidance, or by superior malice, which was invariably assumed by Frau Jansen; a sharp and shrill temper and voice dividing, and disposing of, the more substantial threats and bellowings of her larger-half, as a sharp rock or breakwater divides a tempestuous sea. Now, this remedy completely failed. Neither was he communicative, nor cared more for Mrs Jansen's sarcasms, or temptations to talk, than he did for his daughter's tears. Nothing had disturbed this social suspense at the old farm but the arrival and departure of Harold Falcon. From the time of his visit, as we have seen it to take place, things had gone on better. Jansen had improved by becoming perfectly quiet, but invincibly obstinate. The frau was cheerful, but preferred to appear only resigned. The girl's virtue consisted in a forced hypocrisy, which was, however, confined to her own chamber, as heretofore.

'Margaret, you are prepared to go with me to-morrow?' said Bernhard Jansen on the day and about the time that Harold Falcon was going about London to see friends and provide for his journey on the morrow. He did this after his visit to Lord Hawkestone.

'Yes, father,' said the girl, dropping her hand listlessly, with her work, into her lap. 'Am I going for long?'

'That's impossible for me to tell. Take what luggage you think most needful for immediate use. The best of your wardrobe; what trinkets you have; books that you care about—nothing more. We start from Oxford to-morrow morn-

ing, and in the evening shall be on board the
boat.'

'And you have made up your mind—,' re-
joined the girl.

'Thoroughly. No more, Margaret; remember your promise, the prize, and our word.'
With which Jansen, profoundly grave, left his
daughter's room.

It was a curious coincidence, at all events,
that old Jansen and his daughter left England
on the very day that we must lose sight of Harold
Falcon for a time. One of the most comfortable
assurances that can be held out to men of the
world, that is, of Harold Falcon's world, is the rapidity with which they and their affairs pass out
of mind. We all of us trouble ourselves a great
deal too much about what is thought of us, or
will be thought of us, by those with whom we
daily associate. We need be under little appre-
hension, when we are once gone, that it will re-
quire more than a given number of days to be forgotten. And that number is but small. Those
to whom we owe money will probably remember us with some bitterness for a time; but unless we have been superlatively good or superlatively bad, the place we have occupied in the
world's opinion will soon be filled up by other ob-

jects—worthier because they are more tangible.

Harold Falcon, like all young men, judged that his absence would create some speculation, and it did. But when they had talked him over at Tattersall's, at the clubs in which he was known, at Lady Mary Watt Knott's—whose good-looking daughter had a lively recollection of Harold in Rotten Row,—and at a house or two where he had made himself more than commonly agreeable, they let him go quietly down the stream ; and by the end of about three weeks, he might as well have never existed. He had paid his debts like a gentleman (as far as they knew), and that was more than could be said for everybody that disappeared from the surface of society.

'What's become of Harold Falcon, Jonas ?'— Jonas being the nickname of a light-cavalry man about town of a very practical turn.

'Why ? does he owe you any money ?' says Jonas.

'No, not a farthing; but I've not seen him about this season.'

'Where's that tall good-looking cousin of yours, Hawkestone, that used to ride ?'

'He's abroad at present,' says my lord to Harold's friend, Greystone.

'What took him there at this time of year ?'

'Nothing took him there; but there was still less to keep him here, I suppose.'

'Devilish little to keep him anywhere,' mutters his quondam friend, grumpy at having made so little impression on Hawkestone, who was already several paces away from him, and talking to somebody else.

The people who really interested themselves about him were those who never knew him; but who thought it right to be interested about a ruined Guardsman, of any sort, as being on the confines of high life; these were the would-be fashionables of commercial society. 'Two more gone, Jemima Anne,' remarks Barber of the Corn-exchange, sitting down to dinner, and helping his wife to soup: 'Cranstone's dead, destroyed himself; lost forty thousand on the Waterpark steeplechase; it's all in the paper: and that good-looking fellow, Falcon, bolted.'

'Who's he, dear?' inquires Jemima Anne, a matter-of-fact sort of woman.

'Oh, you know—was in the Guards—deuced handsome fellow.'

'What, a friend of yours, dear?'

'Well, not exactly a friend. I knew him quite well though,' he ought to have added, 'by sight,' but he thought it scarcely worth while.

'I'm really very sorry for him, for he was a very good fellow, at least everybody says so.' Nobody had ever mentioned him to Barber that had even a bowing acquaintance with Harold.

The great world ought to be very much obliged by the interest which is taken in it by us little folk, if it did but know it.

When Lord Hawkestone walked down to Tattersall's with the money from Harold to settle his book, which was very easily done, he found the market very little depressed by Lord Cranstone's suicide. The few thousands due had been spread over a tolerably wide surface, and Harold Falcon was the only one who had lost much by him. The Jews had had so much of his money that they must have paid themselves over and over again.

'Captain Childers, were you looking for any one in particular?' said Hawkestone, as he saw that worthy gentleman from Oxfordshire on the look-out.

'Well, for no one very particularly; but Carruthers asked me to arrange one or two of his bets for him, as I was obliged to come up, and he couldn't.' The Flying Childers was quite certain that Lord Hawkestone owed him nothing, nor he him.

'I think I can relieve your anxieties, if you have any;' and walking on one side he took the notes from his pocket-book, and counting them out, that there might be no suspicion of his personal interference in his cousin's affairs, said, 'Captain Falcon called upon me on Saturday, because he was about to leave London yesterday, and asked me to pay you this money for Carruthers; do me the favour to see that it's right.'

'Quite right,' said the Flyer, who was accustomed to deal with such matters, crumpling the notes up, and thrusting them carelessly into his left-hand trowsers pocket. 'I know Carruthers' account from my own by the pockets; I've given him the left and kept the other for my own. They're neither of them full yet:' saying which, he cancelled the bet in Carruthers' book. 'Did you say Falcon had left town yesterday?'

'I did; he intended to go, and I believe he went. He's gone on the continent for a short time.'

'Ah, I'm sorry for him. It was too bad of Cranstone. He ought to have paid first, and then nobody would have said anything about it.' By which Lord Hawkestone learnt that there were two ways of regarding the same thing. It seemed that Harold's sentiments and his own might be the right thing, but were not both in the right place at ' the Corner.'

After this Harold Falcon was soon forgotten by all but his cousin and his family. Lord Falconberg came to town, and with him Lady Helen. One brother was at Woolwich, a good soldier, who had been put in there as usual in those times by favour. Another was at Eton, who could neither spell nor write English nor do the rule of three, but an excellent school-boy, and could make sapphics as fast as a little dog could trot. A third was waiting for ordination, a good man and having a call, as I verily believe, to the family-living, twelve hundred a-year; and likely to make better use of it than if he had come a licentiate from St Abeilles; a good churchman, not as yet given to chasubles and incense, and not deep in Professor Maurice, nor Gladstone's Church Principles.

Lady Helen was a fine, frank, open-hearted girl, very handsome, of a beauty somewhat *prononcé*, as I said before, but with such kind and winning ways, that she mingled with her dignity a charm of manner perfectly irresistible. The impressions she produced were as variable as the temperature; and it was singular that every one of her acquaintance had hit upon a different excellence

by which he or she judged. Her intelligence, with
which no man falls in love, delighted those who
preferred rational conversation; and her sympathy
and tact made her the especial favourite of the
empty young heads that bobbed up and down
nightly to the music of Weippart or König. Cornet
Têteveau used to say, she was the only girl he
ever cared a pin to dance with, for nobody else
ever seemed to understand him, and he was sure
he did not understand them.   Her truth charmed
the honest, her consideration the timid.   She was
as careful of a person's feelings as a well-bred horse
is of stepping upon a fallen rider, and as independent and courageous in defence of her sex or her
order, as a Knight Templar before Saladin at the
lake of Tiberias or at Acre ; and her form and
features were of a kind to give the highest effect
to every sentiment.   Her eyes could flash with
lustrous brilliancy, or smile with a soft subdued
light through their drooping lashes.   Her short
and expressive lip curled with scorn of base actions, closed with determination, or showed the
pearls between with that happy joyousness, which
is the most infectious of all graces.   Her sincerity
was the distinguishing feature of her character
and apparent throughout, but it was tempered

with a forbearance which never permitted it to give offence.

Of course Lord Hawkestone heard from his cousin. As a matter of courtesy it was to be expected, as a matter of business it was necessary. He seldom talked about Harold—never to indifferent persons; only occasionally to his family. Lord Falconberg heard nothing, as it happened, about his nephew's escapades. He knew him to be generally extravagant, borrowing money and betting; but he had never heard of the extent to which Harold's unfortunate extravagancies had carried him. He was very angry when he sold his commission, attributing it rather to a love of idleness, and a wanton vagabond sort of life on town and at Newmarket, than to its real cause—his necessities. And Harold Falcon had so few enemies, one might almost say so many friends, that though they wouldn't, or couldn't, save him from the Jews, they never gave him up to his uncle.

'Where is Harold now, Hawkestone; you know his address?' said Lord Falconberg at a dinner at his own house.

'I know his address, but I can't tell exactly where he is, for the banker at Innsbruck is only authorized to forward his letters. The last I had from him, he was walking through the Bavarian Highlands. He was then at Berchtesgarten, inspecting the König See, and fishing.' Here Lord Hawkestone stopped, thinking he had said enough.

'That's his view of economy. I've no doubt he spends as much there as he does here. He'd much better come back.'

'That can hardly be, my dear father. Here's Bertie Carteret saw him the other day, and says that he was then at Salzburg, living like an anchorite. Bertie,' added he, 'what did you say he was doing?'

'He was living on half-a-crown a day, and travelling on foot everywhere. I dined with him, and he was quite eloquent on the economy of the Tyrol. He says he often gets his breakfast for threepence. He catches his own trout, and has the cooking, coffee, and bread and butter for a few pence. I can easily believe it,' concluded Bertie; 'it's about its value.'

'You're not enthusiastic about scenery, I suppose, Mr Carteret?' said Lady Helen, who listened to this account of Harold with some interest.

'Not when accompanied by stone floors and

a plethora of veal. We got no other meat, and there was not a decent inn out of the beaten track, and not two in it.'

'How came you in the Tyrol so early?'

'I was coming home from Italy, and halted on my way at Salzburg. Finding Harold, I stopped; for he was quite alone—nobody there at this season.'

'How very strange it must seem to my cousin,' said Lady Helen, 'after living as he has done here for so long.'

'Very foolish of him,' said Lord Falconberg. 'Why doesn't he come home; there's plenty of room for him here. Write to him, my dear.'

'Not very foolish, papa; you must see his motive. If he has a hard school to go to, and a hard lesson to learn in it, it's all the better that he should do so now. Let him learn it thoroughly.'

'I should have thought you were the last person to have recommended that course, Helen. I'm sure you'd welcome Harold home—'

'I think Helen was right, sir, nevertheless,' said Lord Hawkestone. 'Depend upon it he hasn't been so happy for years. Here he was always depending upon other people; there he will learn to depend upon himself.'

'And who's going to ride Crusader next

winter, if Harold doesn't come down to Hawkestone?' inquired the peer with some asperity.

'Winter! oh, that's quite a different matter,'
said Hawkestone; 'he'll be home in the autumn,
I should think. If not, Helen will give you leave
to send for him.'

'Helen will do nothing of the kind,' and she
blushed. 'Harold has to take care of himself;
and he seems to me to have set about it at last.
Don't tempt him, Hawkestone, at present; the
cure's not radical.'

'But it's a serious matter for my father,' replied Lord Hawkestone, laughing.

'The best thing my father can do is to give
him or get him some employment. Surely, with
this Ministry, we ought to be able to do something for him.'

'Ah, that's the difficulty, Nelly. Public
business doesn't keep men out of mischief. A
fellow like Harold, whom everybody knows and
likes, is sure to have a book full of caricatures,
and blotting-paper covered with likenesses of his
chief. They do nothing, and the chiefs do less.'

'That's a promising sketch of the executive,
at all events,' said she.

'It's a true one, Lady Helen,' says Bertie
Carteret; 'I know it all. We never do any-

thing. We've a lot who came in on competition. They know everything—or say they do; but they're really as useless, and far less ornamental, than those who belong to the ancient order of Her Majesty's officials.'

'Then, papa, I don't think official life will do for Harold at all. You must make him your agent.'

'That was meant for George, but he's never been heard of since he took his degree,' said Lord Falconberg. 'Does anybody know where he is?'

'He's going to the colonies,' said Carteret again; 'he told me so the other day. He's now at Gray's Inn, but I saw him in the Temple.'

'Which of the colonies is he going to?' asked Hawkestone.

'He didn't say which; but I think Lord Falconberg had better give me the agency,' replied Bertie, laughing at his own impudence.

'You'll find it harder work than drawing caricatures of your chief, Bertie,' said the old lord, helping himself and passing the claret.

Bertie did not have the agency, but continued to caricature the Ministers. He complained much that they were Whigs, as he wanted a change to try his hand on. And the summer went by, and

the London season was past, and Harold still remained abroad. His cousin George went to the
colonies for a time, having got a pretty good ap-
pointment. Goodwood was just over, and Lord
Falconberg had a few visits to pay with his
daughter. After that he meant to join Lord
Hawkestone in Scotland, who was gone salmon
fishing.

CHAPTER XVI.

WITH all the travelling which has taken place since the time of which I am speaking, very few people have visited the country in which Herr Jansen and his daughter were to be found some time after they had left England. The house in which they were living was a small cottage, comfortable to the last degree, for the country in which it was situated; accommodated with English furniture—carpets, curtains, and such matters—unknown even in the better class of houses at that period. It was situated between Cleves and Nimeguen, considerably removed from the high road, in a bit of country partaking of the sandy soil and tree-clad knolls of the former place. In itself it was pretty enough, surrounded by a small garden, and externally decorated with some of the rude attempts at carving which proclaimed Herr Jansen's taste and its own antiquity.

Margaret Jansen's was the same sad but beautiful face as we saw it a short time before in England. Her father's was disfigured just now with sullenness which was not natural to it, and to which his ordinary violence had given place. I have said before that it was a handsome face, but it must be marvellous beauty that is not disfigured by such a temper. His violence was not unbecoming to him as a matter of appearance.

Margaret was knitting. These German and Dutch women, and all who have affinity with them by blood or habitude, will knit till your gall rises at the provoking monotony of their fingers. She sat back in an arm-chair, while her father stood before her in a denouncing attitude, one hand clasping an instrument of his art, the other a drawing, which he seemed to have been studying. The tears were coursing each other down the cheeks of his daughter.

'It's done, and it can't be undone,' said he, menacing her with his hand. 'You have not fulfilled your part of the contract. That you should have returned to your father's house from the church-door, so to speak, by your own folly and obstinacy, is more than I could believe, if I were not here to see it, and to hear you declare it.'

'I could not help it, father. I could not bear it. I knew why he was brought here, why I was brought here; and when I thought of it, the degradation and deceit was more than I could endure.' Her tears flowed afresh.

'You have become squeamish,' replied Jansen, satirically.

'Not till the last moment. But when he became generous; when he told me the truth, and gave me all back again that he might have taken, I could not withhold the truth, and I told him all.' The girl was half choked by her sobs, and could scarcely proceed.

'And he returned you to your home. Who can blame him? not I.' And then Bernhard Jansen looked long and more sadly at her. 'Margaret, if you knew how hard it is for a child to disappoint every hope, to probe every wound, to tear off the rags that hide, without healing, the cicatrice of a parent, you would not wonder at the revulsion of feeling that would put away the sight of what it once most loved. All my life long I have wanted sympathy. My fellow-workmen scarcely understood me when a boy; your mother was less careful of me than of my house; I looked to you, Peggy,'—and here Margaret got up and threw her arms round the huge old man,

and leant her head upon his breast,—'I watched
you, I indulged you, I listened to your wishes, I
made money, or tried to do so, by unworthy
means, for you. No one sympathized with my
failures; and you cared nothing for my successes.
You cared for others; for their smiles and ap-
proval. You loved admiration, and the world,
and see what it has brought you: and then when
I would have done, have done all for you, to my
shame and discredit you turn round upon me
and thwart the scheme, on which you promised
ready obedience.'

'My father, I tried to obey you—to keep my
word—but I couldn't do it. He was too generous; he spoke openly and honestly, and kindly,
but not affectionately, and—and—'

'You told him—what? that you could not
love him, nor live with him, that your heart—'

'No, father, I told him what was right to tell
him, enough to bring me here again—where I
may live with you, father, and with my mother;
and where I may see no more of the world's
gew-gaws, nor look for more admiration or want
more love than yours.' With which words she
looked up into the eyes of old Bernhard Jansen,
who could scarcely see her through the mist that
covered them. Then, for the first time for many

a long day, he took his daughter in his arms, and kissed her tenderly; and putting her once more in her seat, he walked steadily out of the room.

From that day Peggy's indiscretions were forgiven, if not forgotten, by her father.

With regard to Harold Falcon himself, his friend Bertie Carteret had told nearly the truth. He was living the life of an anchorite, for him. It is only the life, however, which is led by thousands who can afford nothing better, but whose will it is to wander a certain number of weeks of every year at every possible inconvenience. He moved from place to place, carrying his knapsack, and sending his baggage by the great routes. There were no railroads then, and he trusted to the great Flemish horses, or the mules, or the Eilwagen, to supply him with occasional changes.

He could not have passed through a more sudden and incomprehensible difference, had he plunged from the heat of a vapour-bath into the baths at Chamouni, and they are the coldest I remember to have felt. He had in one fortnight dissipated an idle dream, which seemed as though it ought to last for ever, and exchanged for a healthy, active, economical, and utterly useless

existence, the refinements of high society, and
the vices of luxury, idleness, selfishness, and de-
pendence, amid which he was only saved from
utter reprobation by the instincts of an English
gentleman.

There he was, however, walking from mountain to mountain, living at whatever hotel, or
auberge, presented itself; economizing his scanty
allowance, and—luxury of luxuries!—paying for
what he had.

As the summer advanced, he began to be
bored by the succession of visitors who poured
into the *table d'hôtes,* and amongst whom he
could not help meeting occasional friends, as in
the case of Bertie Carteret. Harold had no great
spirits to encounter loud acclamations of recognition from men who had forgotten his existence,
till they saw him: and the pleasure of joining
them had become questionable, the profit nil,
when they talked of a rubber, devilled kidneys, and oceans of claret, as the purest luxuries
of a continental life. Not that the exodus from
this country at all resembles what it is now in
quantity and quality, but there were adventurous
spirits who thought the Swiss mountains were
worth exploring, and who endeavoured to make
English habits dominant among foreign materials.

It was very seldom indeed that Harold was

induced to join any particular party of this kind
for more than an hour or two. His great objec-
tion was the additional expense which he could not
afford, and the determination to be independent
in his movements. It must be admitted that
after some days, perhaps hours, Harold's old
associates would have found him duller than
formerly. That peculiar elasticity of mind was
gone. His debts and his difficulties had depressed his spirits, and made him think: a habit
for which he had seldom had credit given to him,
among the very liberal supplies of that article,
which had been working his ruin. There were
plenty of people, however, estimable people too,
who would have preferred Harold as he was, to
Harold as he had been; but these were of the
steady kind, not given to devilled kidneys and
oceans of claret.

It so happened that Harold Falcon had retired upon Munich, as a place in which he might
winter. The autumn was advancing; and what
with the high road to Vienna, and to one of the
Italian passes, it was a not impossible place for
some amusement with its well-known economy.
In those days, it was an admirable winter residence; and Harold Falcon was an admirer of
art in all its forms.

He was at the *table d'hôte* of the principal hotel, having just taken a seat between a Russian officer and a Viennese dowager, when three Englishmen, one of whom he knew intimately, took their seats opposite to him. They were manifestly off a journey, and they were not long in telling Harold where they were come from.

'Oberammergau?' repeated he, after one or two vain endeavours to repeat the word. 'And where is Oberammergau? and what in the name of fortune took you there, Desmond?'

'It's in the Bavarian Highlands,' replies Desmond; 'and a wonderful place it is. Splendid scenery and rather out of the way, so that you won't like it. Accommodation not quite St James's pattern. There's more beer in the place than curaçoa, and more tobacco than either.'

'I'm not frightened, if you'll only tell me where it is, and why I should go there.'

'The best way to reach it is by Starnberg, and from there, on the road to Innsbruck, you turn off in a magnificent valley—the valley of the Ammer. The village itself is enclosed by mountains and not easy of access, and would be a splendid shelter from persevering creditors.'

'If that's the only advantage, I think Munich is equally good.'

'Well, that's not exactly what took me there. I'm great, as you know, at private theatricals, and I heard of a mediæval affair of that sort to be seen only every ten years: it was the life and death of our Saviour represented on the stage! I've been astonished, as you may believe, who know what amateur theatricals sometimes are, but I never expected to see such an extraordinary performance as that of last Sunday.' Here Desmond and his friends rose, as the majority of the company left the room. 'Kellner, another bottle of that excellent Liebfrau milch, and another glass.' They sat down again.

'But, Desmond, that's only a repetition of the old Parisian mysteries or miracle plays, which have been so tritely explained in a late article in the *Quarterly;* and in which Samson dances a *pas seul* with the gates of Gaza on his back, and the Philistines take him prisoner in a quadrille.' Saying which, these young men, having the room nearly to themselves, proceeded to light cigars (bad ones as might be expected from our present knowledge of that article), and continued their conversation with more *empressement* than is fashionable in Pall-mall.

'It's not exactly that, I think. This is the result of a vow by the inhabitants only of this valley in the early part of the seventeenth century.'

'And who are the actors?' inquired Harold.

'The villagers or parishioners themselves. That was a part of the vow in the event of a plague or pestilence ceasing in that particular place.'

'And do you mean that the drama is remarkable for anything but its absurdity?'

'Absurdity is utterly removed from it. To some men it may appear solemnly blasphemous, to others it may be worth critical examination as a Scriptural play, but to neither will it exhibit features of ridicule.'

''Then on my mind, and I am not a puritan at all events, I think the first effect would be produced, unless the acting is bad; in which case the other.'

'It is a remarkable fact, that the acting is singularly good : the effect produced by having seen Pontius Pilate, the night before, with a tremendous German pipe, inviting his customers to fill themselves with Bavarian beer, and by recognizing Judas Iscariot on the morning of representation, as the honest landlord of your own inn, is odd, but it soon wears off in the interest.'

'Interest—isn't it tiresome, monotonous?'

'Monotonous? Have you seen Macready as Coriolanus? I've seen a better Roman in Pontius

Pilate. Have you seen Kean in Shylock? I've seen a better, a more terrible, Jew. And there's a chorus.'

' A chorus—what do you mean ? '

' Why, not such a chorus as ' We are jolly good fellows,' but a Greek chorus, who perform the parts assigned to them by Horace to the music of Bach.'

' And is there nothing revolting in it?' said Harold Falcon once more, who with all his gambling and debts had a just idea of the fitness of things.'

' Did I say nothing?' replied Desmond. ' I won't say nothing, for the sacrament is administered on a stage by a representative of our Saviour; Judas positively hangs himself before your face, and the crucifixion becomes a palpable fact. But you must see it, Falcon.'

' I will,' said Harold—and he did. But when he took leave of Munich for Oberammergau he had little idea of the intelligence that awaited him there.

It will not be necessary to trouble my readers with an account of the most extraordinary performance that can well be conceived. A spectacle in a theatre which so far resembles the classic stage as to be canopied only by the heavens, and to which some four thousand spectators are admitted, who remain unwearied on their seats from about seven in the morning till four in the afternoon, may well bear that epithet. But as Desmond had well said, the conception of the characters, the comprehension of the whole scheme, the delineation of the most mysterious life, death, and resurrection of the as yet incomprehensible, may be called something more than extraordinary. Fancy the Sanhedrim, its arguments, its determination, its refractory members. The social state of Mary and Martha, the last supper, the betrayal, the visible raising on the cross of the actor in these scenes; the unbelief of the multitudes, the gentlemanly indifference of the Roman, the turbulent malice of the Jews, even to the apparent resurrection amid the astounded soldiery. Has it not all been written in the columns of the *Times* newspaper, in the year eighteen hundred and sixty.

It was then on a brilliant morning in September that Harold Falcon found himself at the doors of what we must call the theatre. He was one of several hundreds already waiting to secure a seat. He had arrived by diligence the night before, and, though the accommodation was of the roughest, he did not feel disposed to be very *exigeant.* In a village whose population was four hundred, but had amounted to about as many thousands for this occasion, the effect upon chance passengers, as regarded bed-fellows, might be expected to rival the inconveniences of poverty itself. Tables, chairs, casks, from which the beer had long departed, the bare floor, in many instances without a covering, empty waggons, and the vehicles and conveyances which were to remain ready for to-morrow's exodus, were none without their occupants.

Harold looked in vain for a fellow-countryman; and had he not found a good-natured German who interpreted his French into a Tyrolese *patois*, it is doubtful by what means he would have got anything to eat or drink in a land which appeared to be flowing with milk and honey.

Harold fought his way into what ought to have been a church this same Sunday morning, but which was, as I say, a theatre. The front seats, into one of which he climbed, were protected to a certain extent from the sun by an enormous canopy overshadowing about two-thirds of the spectators, and extending its welcome shade as far as the orchestra. From rain protection seemed not likely to be needed. Some members of the royal family having arrived at the proper time, a great condescension in crowned heads, the drama began.

When Harold Falcon took his eyes off the stage, which he hardly did till the first act was finished (and there were twelve, to say nothing of *entr'actes* and the chorus), he turned them on his neighbour. It was quite clear that Harold was the only Englishman in the place. There was scarcely an upturned face that could be mistaken for the cleanly-shaven type of our countrymen. There were apparently few but Germans; and one of those few was the man who sat next to Harold. He was a young Frenchman, and a gentleman. A Parisian one would say; for the gloves he wore, in this savage valley, though not irreproachably clean, fitted as at that period Frenchmen's gloves only fitted. Harold looked at his face a second time, and their eyes met. There was then no difficulty in getting into conversation, excepting that which may exist between any old Etonian and a gentleman speaking the language of society all over the world. They would have made themselves understood when it was absolutely necessary, but not before—fortunately the Frenchman spoke English. We need not give it with his accent or idiom. It is enough to say that it was even worse than Harold's French.

' *Mais,* it is wonderful ! ' said the Frenchman, shrugging his shoulders.

' You have nothing like this in Paris ? ' said Harold.

' Nothing ; we are not fanatic enough. In Spain—well—something of the kind ; but professional, rather than dramatic.'

' Have you just come from Paris ? ' inquired Harold again, after a few remarks on the business before them.

' No, indeed ; I am going to Munich to-night, as soon as this is over. Four o'clock, I think. I have a caleche, if I can but get horses at Mürnau. I came direct from Switzerland. I was lately at Chamouni.'

' I have been in Chamouni, early in the season,' said Harold, who felt bound to say something between the acts.

' And have ascended Mont Blanc ? All Englishmen think it their duty to ascend a mountain, where there is nothing to be seen and great danger to be incurred.'

' No, indeed, I have not,' and Harold laughed ; ' but I don't know that I should have been deterred by the danger you speak of. It's a very expensive kind of recreation. Besides which, the weather is not favourable at all times.'

'You are right; none but the most experienced
guides should be consulted, and their advice
strictly followed.   Three of your countrymen
would be alive now, fine young men, if they had
listened to their guides.'

'Three have died lately on Mont Blanc?'

Only two days ago.   The day I left Chamouni.
The weather had been apparently splendid; and on
the day before, these Englishmen wished to make
the ascent.   An experienced guide, named Balmat,
came to us the night before (I was to have gone
with them), and showed us in the clear sky, hanging over the mountains, a small white cloud, no
bigger than my hand.'   And he held it out, well-
gloved and small.   'There is risk to-morrow in an
ascent, said he.   All may go well, but there is
risk.   I and my friends declined to go, and we
did all we could to persuade Mr Falcon to remain,
but—'

'Mr who?' said Harold, and his eyes dilated,
and his hand rested on the arm of the Frenchman
with a nervous grasp, as he put the question.

'Mr Falcon,' and he spoke as distinctly as
possible.   'What, you knew him; he was a friend
of yours?   Ah, forgive me,' as he saw Harold's
agitation, who naturally first jumped to the conclusion that his cousin George was the victim of

his own rashness. So satisfied was he of this probability that he forgot to hear the end of the catastrophe. It was sufficient for him that a Mr Falcon had perished on Mont Blanc : there was but one of that name that it could well be.

His mind was made up at once, so he said abruptly,

'You return to Munich at once ?'

'My carriage is ordered at half-past four to-day.'

'The gentleman you mention is a relative of mine. I can get to Chamouni more quickly by reaching Munich or Innsbruck first. You will excuse me if I ask whether you have room, and if so inclination to allow me to share your carriage, should you have room.'

The Frenchman took his hand, and assured Harold of his wish and power to serve him. He had no companions on this part of his journey, and the Englishman's company would be a pleasure to him, and a great advantage : you know the road?' It was kindly said.

'I know you must go to a place called Mürnau from here ; and then to the lake of Starnberg. The road to Munich is well known from there, and we shall reach it late to-night or early to-morrow morning.'

'That will depend upon the horses,' inquired the Frenchman.

'Whether we can get them? At a time like this there may be difficulties.'

'Then let us be off at once. Anything to relieve your anxieties.'

'No, no, monsieur,'—and Harold insisted upon his friend remaining to the last scene,—'after that as soon as you will.'

The journey to Munich was a difficulty from the crowded state of the road. First, was the caleche forthcoming? There it stood, ready and packed, and Harold threw in his knapsack, and was ready to be gone. He fidgetted to a degree. Then came the horses. The landlord was willing to assist the Frenchman, reminiscent of old alliances (for he had been a soldier), and he put the horses to, with Harold's assistance. But where was the post-boy—the Kutscher? Where was the best Bavarian beer to be found? And while Harold bit his lip, and thought over the terrible catastrophe, he could not ask his companion to recount the story. At last came the Kutscher, and they started.

But when men are in a hurry they always seem to be delayed. Not that really they are so, but their thoughts so far precede their actions, as to throw the latter needlessly into the background. The crowd was not greater at the dirty little village, at which they stopped to sup, and bait their cattle on *schwartz-brod*, than was always the case on such occasions; but Harold's mind was at Munich, anxiously inquiring for letters, long before his body could be so. The steamer on the lake at Starnberg was no later than usual, nor were they longer in getting the caleche on board than they should have been, but Harold Falcon had not been accustomed to contradiction or delay, and the present seemed to him an occasion when there ought to have been none. He swallowed his food as if bad digestion was an acceleration of speed; and when at last he reached Munich, he was disposed to blame the government that he had still some few hours, in which he must refresh himself after his journey.

His fellow-traveller, Alphonse de Castelnau, flattered himself that he had acquired the *sang-froid* which was supposed to be purely British, that he had in fact supplanted his companion in that desirable characteristic.

'Did you hear, Monsieur de Castelnau, who were the companions of Mr Falcon in his ascent.'

'No, indeed, I did not. The principal was a

Mr Falcon; those who accompanied him were younger. He seemed to have the management of them. They lived together the only two days I was with them, and arranged the intended ascent among themselves.'

This was but little like George, unless he had taken pupils with him from Oxford or London, thought Harold. And then he proceeded to catechise his companion, who to tell the truth was well disposed to gratify his curiosity.

'Tall, I think you say?' And to show how much his mind was occupied with his subject, he asked the question *a propos* to nothing.

'Yes, and rather dark, but not so dark as you.' Saying which, the young Frenchman looked at Harold, and tried to trace a likeness, but failed. Then he ventured to ask for particulars. 'They had been watched from the Breven; everything had gone right even to the *grands et petits mulets:* but the atmosphere had become clouded, the wind had risen, the summer heat had loosened the frozen snow from its base, and an avalanche from which there was no escape had carried down the three·Englishmen and a guide, the rest having been miraculously preserved; they themselves knew not how.'

Harold arrived at Chamouni at last, not by our

modern method of railway travelling, but by the
monotonous and circuitous route of divers eil-
wagens, which, if pace have anything to do with
it, certainly do not deserve the name. He had
written to his banker at Vienna, and received
supplies, which met him at one point of his
journey ; for he felt that it would be necessary to
husband his resources for the melancholy event
in which he was to participate. There was no
doubt of its truth, and an interview with the
first stranger he met, left no doubt on his mind
of the truth of a portion at least of the Frenchman's story.

The man who reaches a place unexpectedly,
bearing the same name as one who has just been
destroyed by an avalanche, unless it be Smythe
or Jones, is sure of some sort of recognition. He
must excite some feeling, either of curiosity or
envy, perhaps of compassion. The aubergiste
was all attention, and detailed as much as he
knew of the adventure. ' *The* three gentlemen
had met with this untimely fate '—he said that in
English, having learnt much of that language
from books. He added the expressive word
' schrecklich' from his own. Would Monsieur
like to see the visitors' book, and the English
chaplain. The first was in the house, the second

in his lodgings, not a stone's throw from the hotel.

'Yes,' said Harold, 'I should like to see the visitors' book; but not here. Allow me to come to your private apartment.'

'With pleasure, Monsieur,' and the waiter led the way. Before he left the public-room, into which he had been shown, Harold looked round. There were a few Englishmen there, not one of whom he knew; a few who might have been English had they not been Americans. There was nobody immediately present to whom he felt disposed to talk, so he followed the waiter.

He was scarcely prepared for the surprise. He ran his finger down the book in the page presented to him by the landlord, who stood aloof, and stopped at the word 'Falcon.'

The Hon. Jervoise Falcon.

'*Si, Monsieur;* that's the gentleman who was here, and is—' The man did not finish the sentence. Harold's finger continued along the line, —'and brothers.'

'The Hon. Jervoise Falcon and brothers,' repeated he to himself, scarcely able to articulate the words; 'my cousins—poor Helen!' The book remained open before him.

'And those were the gentlemen who were with you?'

'They were. They made the ascent together. They waited here some days before they could ascend, and then, *ach Gott!*' And the poor landlord, who had the feeling of landlords usually for lost customers, and some for customers lost altogether, spread his hands and ceased speaking.

'Der Herr Pastour von Schmidt!' said the waiter at this juncture opening the door. This high-sounding title ushered in a quiet, well-bred gentleman, clothed in coloured trowsers, a black coat and waistcoat, and a white neckcloth, who answered to the name of Smith. He was the clergyman of the English congregation at Chamouni during the summer and autumn months. Such an institution was quite novel then; it has become necessary now. However, we may presume without offence that it is not the Smiths who have brought the congregations, but the congregations who have brought the Smiths. I wish well to the labours of that energetic class during the Paris Exhibition. There will be great need of their labours, and much opportunity for their exertions, if I know anything of the attractions of that capital.

A word on Herr von Schmidt, who presented himself to Harold as the English chaplain, anxious to sympathize with a sufferer, and to offer his assistance in any way that it could be made available. Smith had no fault in the world but one. He found it quite impossible to make both ends meet upon seventy-five pounds a year and a cottage in a healthy and picturesque part of Hampshire. He had a wife and three children; and he was obliged to wash, dress, and eat and drink—the whole lot of them upon that miserable pittance—as a gentleman ought to do. He lasted as long as he could in an ungrateful country which knows no crime equal to poverty, in a social point of view. He had taken three years' credit, after paying away all the ready money he could raise, and then disappeared among the savage rocks, crevasses, and glaciers of a country which, as Smith poetically observed, was less inhospitable than his own. Even there, he scarcely contemplated remaining longer than necessity and his landlord's claims demanded. Beyond this incapability to support life (not his own alone) upon nothing, men knew of nothing to his prejudice.

Mr Smith was not long in explaining to Harold everything it was necessary for him to know. There was no doubt as to the fact that the unhappy Englishmen were Harold's cousins, Lord Falconberg's sons. They had come abroad after the beginning of the Eton vacation; and as few

better opportunities could have presented themselves, under the guidance of Jervoise, the two
boys—one of nineteen, the other nearly two
years younger—had started for Switzerland. An
ascent of Mont Blanc has become a matter of
every day's occurrence in these times of muscular
Christianity and universal athletics. At that time
it was a feat no more difficult than now, but
bringing with it just that amount of increased
glory which is due to the increased expense.
Even then, however, unruly spirits were unwilling
to take advice, or to govern themselves by that
experience, which, if it ever is peculiarly valuable,
is so in the latitude of the high Alps.

It is somewhat curious that, in a thoroughly
selfish, worldly-minded spendthrift, it was some
hours before he remembered the difference that
these most untimely deaths made to his own
prospects. He thought of Helen and of his uncle;
and it was not till Mr Smith, in the plenitude of
his snobbism, reminded him of it, that he saw
how much more terrible this accident must appear than if it had happened to the three sons of
a poor old apple-woman, whose absolute bread
depended upon their existence; as if natural
affection were not always swallowed up in the
practical utility of one's offspring.

'Sons of Lord Falconberg, I believe, Mr Falcon,' said the Herr Pasteur; 'always so distressing when such a loss befalls our aristocracy.' And Smith turned the cigar in his mouth, which if worse was cheaper than those he smoked at Cambridge. 'The loss of an eldest son must be a terrible blow in such a family as yours.'

'But this gentleman was not Lord Falconberg's oldest son; though I think my uncle and the rest of the family will feel it terribly.' And then it first occurred to Harold, that three days ago there stood four good lives between him and the title, and now but one. He was sure, at least, that it would be welcome intelligence to Messrs Meshech and Co.'

'Ah, how fortunate!' said Smith, as if they could therefore be well afforded; 'and you will proceed to London immediately. I have already seen the authorities here on the subject; and anything, as a relation, you should wish to be done, shall be carried out to the letter. I mean as to their effects. I fear there is no hope that they, poor fellows, will ever be recovered.'

CHAPTER XVII.

THE PRODIGAL RETURNS.

THERE was nobody in town that could possibly
be out of it. There was Bond-street half up, St
James's-street was in its usual condition of gas-
fitting, and Pall-mall was boarded and hoarded
from the Athenæum to the Guards' Club. The
National Monuments were being cleaned, and
another figure was being talked of for Trafalgar-
square, but nothing was being done. All the
men that one knew were in Scotland, i.e. about one
hundred per cent. of those that are there now ; all
the watering-places on the South-coast were full ;
Scarborough had just bought three bath-chairs ;
and St Leonards had succeeded in entrapping an
earl and two baronets with their families for a
month. The West-end looked as if the veriest
mauvais sujet might have traversed it with nothing
for idle hands to do.

The sun shone down upon the baked pave-
ments, the winds blew up and down the streets,

the dust took possession of the shop windows and
counters, for there were none to retard its pro-
gress by either a watering cart or a duster.
There was one waiter at Long's, John Collins
reigned alone at Limmers', two clerks managed
the business at Herries and Farquhar's, while a
single partner sat in the back parlour studying
the *Morning Post* for an account of Lord Blazing-
ton's success among the grouse, and one solitary
member, Boreham, had the whole of White's
window to himself.

It was late in the day when a post-chaise and
a pair of horses which were smoking with the last
stage of the Dover-road drove up to the Clarendon.
At that well-appointed house there was a porter,
who however felt that it must be a mistake, and
was about to close that portal upon the chaise,
when he happened to catch sight of the occupant.
He touched his hat and advanced to the window.

'Will you inquire whether anything has been
left here for me, or whether Lord Falconberg has
been in town lately?'   The man retired, and
returned in a minute.

'A letter was sent from here to Lord Falconberg only yesterday, sir: so that the clerk does
not think his lordship will be in town again yet.
His lordship went down to Hawkestone from

here. The house in Grosvenor-square is shut up, sir.'

'Thank you; tell him to drive on to Limmers'.' And he did so.

At the moment the chaise turned into Conduit-street, Harold—for it was he—caught sight of Lord Billesdon, an old acquaintance, and intimate with his cousin Hawkestone. His lordship not only knew everybody, but all things. If anybody could give him information, it would be he.

'Billesdon,' said Harold, alighting opposite to him, or rather waiting till he reached the corner of St George's-street, 'how came you to be in town?'

'Not by choice, Harold. Did you ever see such dust: I'm just back from Halliburton's. The worst of the heather is that it unfits one for any other sort of walking. I can hardly get on on level ground without tumbling down.' And here Lord Billesdon indulged in a laugh.

'Good sport?'

'Excellent. Halliburton didn't shoot himself; but Spencer Pole did.'

'Good heavens, Billesdon, what do you mean?'

'Oh! I see—rather good that. I mean, did

not shoot—himself, you know? We were generally two parties of three guns each, and he wasn't
with us. Hawkestone was there—he left us two
or three days ago. Egad! I see you've heard the
news, by your hat. Awful! wasn't it?'

'It was—then they know it at Hawkestone.
I was half afraid they had never heard it: and
was going to post down to-night.'

'Yes. It was in the papers. Now I think of
it, it's a pull for you. It's an ill wind that blows
nobody good.' Harold didn't answer his very
obvious congratulations; but ordered a bed at
Limmers'. Having wished Lord Billesdon good-
bye, and declined his club-dinner, he performed
his ablutions and went out.

Whenever a man is bent upon shirking one
bore, or upon having a quiet hour's digestion,
mental or physical, he may be quite certain that
a moral Charybdis awaits him in the shape of
another. And so it was with Harold Falcon upon
this occasion. It may easily be conceived that he
had plenty of subjects on which to exercise his
meditations; and with a knowledge of the deserted
state of London it was not extraordinary that he
sought the solitude he wanted at his club.

To all appearance he found it. The huge
room was deserted, the handsome curtains, mir-

rors, and chandeliers were covered with brown holland, and one only servant with a third or fourth day's pair of stockings on, and a generally dirty tone, was to be found sitting disconsolately over the evening paper. He looked almost happy when Falcon asked what he could have for dinner, and presented a carte which had not been changed since the functionary's shirt. Having ordered what he wanted and taken his choice of tables, he walked out for half an hour.

'Well, Meshech,' said Harold, walking into the dingy back room of a dirty house in Oxendon-street, which had externally the appearance of a lawyer's office, but was in reality a bill-discounters' den of thieves,—'good-morning. I'm come to England with some foreign money, and I want to change it. I'm going back to the club, and you can do it at once.

'With pleasure, captain,' said Meshech, bowing in a fashion to Harold which was quite new to him; 'with pleasure, and what's the figure, captain?'

There's a rouleau, there's another, that's eighty pounds. Here are half-a-dozen Napoleans, at sixteen and eightpence; and these are five-franc pieces. I know you'll give me the best exchange.'

'Moses! why should I give *you* the best exchange? I should give the best to everybody. There, captain, there's the money. You've been away in the country somewhere.'

'I have, since I saw you. I think we're all safe now, Meshech. Nothing out against us?'

'Nothing out against us, captain, assuredly. And you don't want anything in my way? Times are better, and I can afford a hundred at moderate rate.'

'That's more than you could a twelvemonth ago, Meshech. You've become wonderfully liberal all of a sudden,' said Harold.

'Ah, liberal—well, you're an old friend, Captain Falcon; but money's very dear, very tight: there's the whole of the regiment always a renewing.'

'I can do without now, for the present that is. But I say, Meshech, do you remember your offer a long time ago—two thousand down for the reversion of Hawkestone Castle and the estates?' And Harold couldn't help looking somewhat maliciously at the old Jew, who shrieked out,

'Yes! yes! I'll do it now; take three thousand—there, that's handsome, captain; you know there's four good young lives between you and Hawkestone.' But any one who had looked at the

Jew might have detected some *arrière pensée*. Harold only smiled and said,

'I'm afraid you've been muddling your brain by reading the papers, old man; there, don't be angry. You see I know all about it.' Saying which Harold walked through the murky passage, and disappeared.

His dinner was ready, and all the better for being undisturbed. He had got to the lemon pudding, which he thought safe, and knew to be good, when a Colonel Mullingar walked into the dining-room, and took the seat next to him.

Colonel Mullingar was an Irish gentleman of good position, in parliament, chairman of quarter sessions, and up to his eyes in horseflesh. Just one of those men it is impossible to get rid of. He had also the tenacity of the leech, when he once drew blood.

'Falcon, bedad! is it you? Ah, this is pleasant now; and nobody in London that fool of a waiter said. What's the committee about that they keep such a fellow? Well, now, and how have you been?'

Falcon groaned inwardly, but smiled like all martyrs—it's the right thing to do. 'Thank you, pretty well.' Here the lemon pudding ought to have been sent away, but he began to eat again

in self-defence. Unfortunately the colonel was
one of those men whom it is impossible to shunt;
he was so respectable that it did men good to be
seen with him even; so that it would never do
for Harold to retreat; besides he had ordered
cheese and a salad and a pint of Burgundy, *Clos
Vougeot.*

'What's doing in the country, colonel? I've
been abroad.'

'The ministers are performing just now on
the provincial stage. They prognosticate great
things for the people, which are to cure all their
ailments : household suffrage, or manhood suffrage; the universities thrown open to the Non-
conformists, excepting the Romanists—which is
intended to gratify my countrymen; an increase
of the Episcopate, without a seat in the Lords; the
abolishment of capital punishment, and the Lord-
lieutenancy of Ireland ; and the total abolition of
the game-laws.

'By Jove, colonel, those are sweeping measures. I presume they intend some of these measures to be gradual at all events.'

'Faith, sir, I don't know what we're coming
to. I've a helper in my stables that can't clean
a horse; but he can read and write and do the

rule of three.   And where do you come from just now—from Hawkestone ? '

' From Chamouni, to-day, with some melancholy news for my uncle.'

' We've heard of it.   The old lord will suffer, Falcon; it's a sad business, what with Lady Helen's engagement, and Hawkestone's ill-health.' .

This was news to Harold; and he was so surprised that he repeated the old colonel's words—
' Lady Helen's engagement ! '

' Why, haven't you heard ?   The finest girl in London engaged to that d—d fool, Farina.'

' And Hawkestone's ill-health.   What's the matter with Hawkestone ? '

' Matter enough, my dear fellow.   He hasn't six months to live.   Cardiac has given him up, and Dr Lobel thinks he may last two years in Madeira, with luck.   With luck, mind you.'

Harold was not a man of brusque manners, far from it ; but he took up his hat, and wishing the colonel a good evening, just as that worthy began to think that he had roused some sort of interest in his hearer, disappeared down the stairs, and walked slowly to his hotel.

By the first particular conveyance out of town the next morning Harold Falcon took an outside place for Hawkestone. John Collins, that elaborate compounder of whisky punch (Stultz had his rivals in coats, Golby in breeches, but John Collins was unrivalled in punch), who had known the captain in his palmiest days, was somewhat scandalized by his proceedings. Nothing short of a chaise out and pair would have satisfied him; and he was not quite sure that the captain should have gone away from Conduit-street with less than four. However, as it was clear to Harold that he was saved from the pain of carrying such heart-rending intelligence, he felt the necessity of posting down the road to be less than that which urged him up to town from Dover. Indeed he was not very sorry to delay the meeting with his uncle and cousin; for he knew it would be a painful one whenever it occurred; and the only bit of selfishness which peeped out of his character was his sincere pleasure at not being the first bearer of the melancholy news.

He reached the lodge-gates of Hawkestone Castle, and leaving his luggage made his way on foot to the house. The servants who opened the door to him were already in their mourning, and an air of stillness, quite unusual with a place in which so much gaiety and life had usually prevailed,

proclaimed the change that had come over it.
When he reached the top of the magnificent staircase, which led to a room generally in use when
the family were alone, the servant threw open
the door and announced ' Mr Falcon.'

In a moment Hawkestone was on his feet;
and walking up to his cousin, shook him warmly
by both hands; while Lady Helen rose from her
chair and made no attempt to conceal her satisfaction.

' I knew it. I was sure this great grief would
bring Harold back to us.'

It was in his uncle that the young man saw
the great change that a few days' grief will sometimes bring to the old. The bereavement of his
sons had shaken the old lord; and when Harold
sought him in his sanctum he found him unable
to conquer his emotion. The fine old sportman's
cheeks had not the fresh bright complexion,
which, with his white silken hair, was the characteristic of his face; and the clear gray eye and
well-shaped features were drawn and lined, and
seemed not yet to have recovered their serenity.
Harold had been a great favourite of Lord Falconberg, until his habits of dissipation and his
taste for gambling had somewhat alienated his
uncle's affection for him; and he had never for-

given his imprudence or independence in leaving the Guards. Now he was glad to see Harold, and to welcome him again. Something unusual mingled with the tenderness with which he received him, and he seemed to think that the affection—the objects of which he had lost—might well be bestowed upon his old friend Harold.

Harold Falcon himself could not help being flattered by the kindness of his uncle and Hawkestone. But Lady Helen's expressions of confidence in him were inexpressibly dear to him. She understood him; she saw through all his vanity and extravagance that he was not the selfish being that almost every one must give him credit for being. And as we cling with the greater tenacity to the one remaining support when the rest have betrayed us, so did Harold see in his cousin one connecting link with what he had been, but could scarcely hope to be again.

Before leaving this part of our story, I should be glad to leave as good an impression of our hero on the reader's mind as possible. For this purpose it will be necessary to consider his antecedents, and compare with them the present condition of mind at which he has arrived.

The law of primogeniture, a remarkable law, which furnishes us with stalwart gentlemen of ample means and good report capable of keeping up their state, and improving their tenantry, had borne with a little weight on the Falcon family. The owner of Hawkestone and the title of Falconberg had a clear rentroll of about thirty thousand a-year—certainly enough to live upon like a gentleman. The younger brothers of this family had, however, been but slenderly provided for, excepting by that beneficent providence which a scandalous world calls jobbery. The father of Harold—General Falcon—and of a numerous offspring who have nothing to do with this story, was in the army. He had lived a jovial, rollicking life at home, riding the family horses to the family hounds, and drinking the family claret and champagne to the health of himself and the rest of the neighbourhood. Once in the army, as the cadet of a fine old Tory family with a vast amount of influence and will to serve the Government, he was not allowed to want for anything that patronage could give him. And why not? It had been and still was in the nature of things. But after the general's death, when these good things returned to that villanously-reformed House of Commons, what was to be done with his boys? There was a dirty little incompetency for each, which served to give them bread and

cheese and beer, instead of clear turtle and champagne, and the pleasure of walking for a constitu-
tional after a heavy day's work was done, instead
of Flint, the keeper, with Falconberg's pointers,
or the chestnut mare, and the young Irish horse,
to ride through the early part of the day. Harold
had enjoyed all this to perfection. There was
nothing he couldn't do during his father's life,
and nothing he didn't want after his father's
death. He had all the tastes of a fast man, all
the feeling and instinct of a disappointed one.
Thrown into the best society, how was he to keep
pace with it. Crockford's and Newmarket presented the only resources available for a gentleman. Then came debt, and the means of paying
for a certain time was obvious; so long as his
commission was not forestalled, the Jews were
merciful. If ever any man had been well treated
it was Harold Falcon, but it could not last for
ever. Like all gamblers, sometimes he was lucky,
sometimes the reverse. A splendid horseman,
and a friend of many owners (who by-the-way are
very bad judges of their horses' capabilities),
Jansen and such men would trust to his pulling off
a good stake, before the fatal *trimestre* was over.
A fine, handsome, unquestioning borrower, regardless of percentage or the price of money, he

was a favourite with many, who would rather have given him a turn than many a better man.

With such temptations is it wonderful that he came to grief? His uncle's allowance and his pay would have kept a poor man's son honestly; it procured for Harold gloves (which were then accustomed to be worn outside of the pockets), an opera stall, a modest hack or two with good knee action, which he kept at livery; rooms in the Albany, the entrée at a few good clubs, the best clothes, boots, and cigars in London, with all the other necessaries of existence; to which having been always accustomed, he considered himself still entitled. How he managed to go on so long no one seems to know. The sale of his commission was a mistake; but Hawkestone, who tried to dissuade him, was powerless. He knew his own necessities best, he said; and his cousin offered him assistance, which he would not accept because he knew it to be useless. Then came his last *coup*, by which he might have lasted another year or two, but which happy device was destroyed by the suicide of poor Lord Cranstone. Then he went abroad.

So far Harold had been a fool, and worse, he had been a gambler and a *roué*, but there was some good in him yet. He got hold of some

money, enough to leave England; it is not our
business here to ask how.   Jansen was satisfied,
so was Harold, but he didn't look so.   From
that moment, however, Harold Falcon formed a
resolution of amendment from which he never
swerved.   We must follow him now through
other phases of his life; he has learnt his lesson
without any hard teaching, and it may be that
something severer would be better for him, perhaps is in store for him.   We have but slight
experience of his capability to bear the pressure
of long overgriping poverty, still less of his forti-
tude in unexpected success.

CHAPTER XVIII.

HAWKESTONE CASTLE.

THERE are certain parts of the north-western provinces of England which appear to me to combine all the beauties of scenery requisite for completing a finished landscape. Wood, water, verdant uplands interspersed with the golden grain, are there united in one picture; while the rich and fertile meads are broken in upon by a wilder scenery, partaking in a measure of the sterner character of the Welsh Principality.

It was in one of these counties that Hawkestone Castle was situated. It had long been the property of the Falcon family, who had, indeed, no other seat in England belonging to them. So that the time which was not spent at a favourite shooting-lodge in Aberdeenshire and the London house in Grosvenor-square, was devoted to Hawkestone. And here was dispensed that princely hospitality so becoming our English nobility, and so far distinguishing them from any other aristocracy. Here it was that assembled not only the old lord's county friends, the astute politicians or faded courtiers of the Regency and Carlton House, the old sportsmen who still rode with the Hawkestone, or went in their four-in-hand barouches to the county meetings, but the young Guardsmen and men-about-town, who drank Lord Hawkestone's claret at his club, and indulged in the same Greenwich and Richmond dinners as he and Harold. It was at Hawkestone Castle that, while the elders plotted new Reform Bills, to be given or withheld, who speculated upon the probability of a Whig or Tory Government, many a match over four miles of fair hunting country, or the last half of the Abingdon mile at Newmarket, was concluded: and while the steady rubber for shillings and fives was going on in the blue drawing-room, the billiard-room was kept alive by a flow of wit, conversation, and high spirits which would have been looked for in vain in any other house in the county. Hawkestone was essentially *the home* of the Falconbergs, and to all the neighbourhood, and to all their friends, it opened its portals in the true charity of a feudal gentleman. If the great were welcomed by the lordly hospitality of its owner, the poor man was never allowed to forget one object for which so many blessings were bestowed upon his master.

From one of the grandest situations that can be conceived in a country like this, where beauty is rather the characteristic of the landscape than its greatness, Hawkestone Castle looked down upon a vale rich in every variety of scenery; and on to distant hills and wooded promontories, each of which served for an especial landmark in their several counties or neighbourhoods. Some portion of no less than seven different counties were said to be seen from the Castle terrace; and the whole prospect, on one side at least, was enhanced by the broad and rapid river, which lost itself miles and miles from the Castle, after wandering as a silver cord through its banks; here gently sloping to meet the current, and there boldly defying it with massive rocks and steep or rugged sides; while it appeared like a chain which linked the whole together, and formed a bond of union and beauty almost as much in fact as in idea. Where many a stream has, like the Rubicon or the Rhine, separated interests and prompted strife, the noble stream, which was seen for miles from Hawkestone, was a by-word of love and strength between those who dwelt upon its banks.

The immediate neighbourhood of the Castle is

worthy a closer description. The building itself
was so far remarkable that that part of it which
was inhabited was no more a castle than Buck-
ingham Palace. It was a very large, massive,
cheerful-looking structure, which had been built
of a grey stone in the reign of Charles, or more
strictly speaking, during the Commonwealth,
the previous building having been burnt during
the Civil War. There remained, however, a certain portion of the old building, a magnificent
tower and façade, to which the more modern
portion had been added; thus securing to the
present edifice the name which it had borne since
the days of William II., in whose reign it was
built. On three sides it was surrounded by a
magnificent terrace, in the centre of which were
fountains and basins, with a succession of closely-
kept lawns and beautiful flower-beds, rich during
the summer with every colour that science or
wealth could devise and procure. The third side
was devoted to the offices, forming a large and
imposing quadrangle, of which three sides were
stables, approached by lofty gateways on either
side, on which were the old badges and coats of
arms of the worthy and earliest warriors of the
family. Descending from the terrace, in itself a
long promenade extending round three sides of

the Castle, by succeeding steps and terraces, on the pedestals of which appeared again colossal statues of the favourite emblem—a falcon with outstretched wings and golden claws—the explorer came upon an abrupt hill or knoll, leading to the river's side, through shrubberies and walks planted throughout with rhododendrons, azalias, and other American shrubs; while here and there rare and valuable pines and foreign firs served to enrich the beauty and prodigality of nature. On the right stretched the park, on the near side of the river, undulating soberly, and interspersed with occasional patches of wild heather; while on the other side, woods 'in gay theatric pride' came down to the very edge of the stream, ascending higher and higher as they retreated from the banks, until they rose, in places, almost to a corresponding height with the Castle.

It was here that Lord Falconberg had his *battues*. Here he bred innumerable pheasants, among the gnarled oaks which twisted their giant limbs on either side of the river. Here too the vixen laid up her cubs in the dry sandy soil, and brought them down in the spring and early summer to drink; until in the morning, when the heavy dew was still upon the grass, the young hounds were thrown in to learn their lesson, and

to move the foxes destined for the winter's sport.
In these covers was the flight of the woodcock
stayed, and many a couple in December rewarded
Lord Hawkestone and his friends for the trouble
of a walk through the tangled briars and bram-
bles of the Hawkestone covers: which, indeed,
reminds me that I may have an opportunity of
correcting some mistaken notions on the subject
of *battue* and cover shooting, which appear to
belong mainly to those who can have no experience of its virtues, necessities, or difficulty.
Here, too, beneath these woods reposed the silvery
salmon in its pool, a rare victim to the skill and
perseverance of Harold Falcon, when, as a boy,
he preferred the society of the old keeper, with
his rich store of anecdote and sport, to the more
sober realities of book-learning. The browsing
deer and the lordly stags that grazed over the
open pasture, or stood at gaze beneath the mould-
ering branches of the decaying oak, gave a finish
to the whole scene, which was one scarcely to be
equalled. Such was the hereditary property of
the Falcons.

The house, in its way, was as beautiful as the
park and grounds. The very colour of the stone
gave a massive warmth to it, which, while it impaired none of its original grandeur, added to it

that sentiment of *home* in which so many of our finest residences are deficient. Some are like barracks, some like infirmaries, some like ogres' castles, and some so overloaded with ornament, or so subdued with stained glass, mullions, fretted roofs, and ecclesiastical gloom, as to make sunshine almost an impossibility, and dancing an impropriety, if not something worse. There was nothing like this in the Castle. It was ample enough for anything. There were huge reception rooms, which might accommodate the county; there were fine airy passages and open corridors and spaces all over the house. The hall upon which we entered was lofty and noble in its proportions; but was warm and cheerful in winter, with the dogs at either end, which supported the crackling logs of pine and elm; and light and cool in summer, with its open windows and bright prospects. From its sides sprung the arches which led into the sitting-rooms on either side; and in the centre was the magnificent staircase, not kept in lavender for the reception of lord-lieutenants, peers, county magnates, or metropolitan grandees, but in ordinary use for the members of Lord Falconberg's family and the guests they entertained habitually.

And in former times, when some old lord was

a younger man, a very jovial, rollicking set those guests were, requiring a good broad staircase to go up and down, and a house in which the noise in the dining-room need not be heard by the countess in the drawing-room. Such things had been in generations gone by; but we write of a day when, if vice is as rampant, it is at least more refined, perhaps more insidious.

The rooms were hung with fine old portraits of the Falcons. Warriors—apocryphal gentlemen, who must have been indebted to imagination for their existence in oil or on canvas, though the scrolls of their fame existed in the Hawkestone archives. Statesmen and men of learning, governors of colonies, soldiers, sailors, and fine gentlemen, were ranged around the rooms, interspersed with charming portraits of sportsmen of the last age, with hound and horn, which latter, as there represented, required but little winding beyond what the artist had given it. There were two courtiers, as we have said, and country gentlemen of the Sir Roger de Coverley school, who had found the size of the rooms and the width of the staircases more than convenient.

CHAPTER XIX.

AFTER A LONG INTERVAL.

It wanted about an hour or two to dinner at the Castle, and two persons, old acquaintances of the reader, were sauntering leisurely, as it appeared, towards the house. Not so leisurely in mind as in body. Actively, indeed, in that respect, were they both engaged, as they came slowly on by the river's bank towards the steep hill-side, which led to the steps of the terrace.

'And you think my father much altered, Harold?' said Lady Helen, as she waited a moment, while Harold Falcon threw once more among some dark stones, in the hope of a rise, before getting his tackle together.

'I do, very much. He seemed two or three years ago to have almost recovered his spirits after the death of those poor boys in Switzerland; but latterly he looks worse than I have ever seen him. What is it, Helen?'

'You have noticed nothing yourself in any way?' said she, shading her eyes with her hand, as the sun was getting lower in the west, and looking at her cousin with a searching glance.

'Nothing, calculated to give him fresh uneasiness. There can be nothing in his affairs; for though he has always kept a liberal and almost extravagant house, my uncle has such a property as to justify any state he may choose to live in. And as to Hawkestone,'—and here Lady Helen took a more serious and rigid investigation of Harold's face.

'Well, Harold, what of Hawkestone?'

'I don't believe he ever gave Lord Falconberg a moment's uneasiness in his life. I wish to goodness I could say the same.'

'And you regret it, Harold, I'm sure. He was hurt at your leaving the Guards without consulting him, and at some other little matters. But it's so long ago, and circumstances have so altered—I think you would like to do him a favour if you could.' And Lady Helen's voice faltered strangely when she got as far as this; which it need not have done, seeing that they were not only cousins, but had been much together all their lives.

'I don't suppose you doubt it, Helen; but it

sounds like the fable of the Lion and the Mouse ;
that not always struck me as being a very exceptional case, indeed.'

'He talks a great deal about you, when you
are away; and yesterday he told me that he
should like to have you down here constantly.
And, in fact, Harold,'—and Lady Helen spoke
with some little hesitation,—'papa asked me to
mention it to you, and see whether there was any
prospect—'

Harold Falcon never raised his eyes to the
beautiful face by his side, but said—not in the
calm quiet tone in which he usually spoke, but in
a rather quick, unsettled voice—'Constantly? No,
no, he didn't mean constantly. He forgets too,
Helen,'—and here he gave a little laugh, somewhat forced,—'that since our great-aunt's death
I am a landed-proprietor.'

'So I told him.' Here Harold looked at his
cousin curiously, as if he would know the exact
meaning of these words. But Lady Helen did
not flinch. 'So I told him,' said she; 'but he
said you could easily let the place you have, that
it wasn't worth half a year's income of Hawkestone, and that it was better for you to be here.'
Lady Helen said all this quite mechanically, and
gave Harold no sort of idea that she herself was

interested in his movements, either one way or the other.

'Have you any notion that my uncle has a particular reason for such a wish?' Helen blushed deeply, though Harold did not see her; for their thoughts had wandered into different channels; as young men's and maidens' will when the confidence between them can be but partial. At length she said, 'Yes; he wants you to take the active management of the hounds.'

'But there's Hawkestone. Surely he's as good for the purpose as I.'

'And the covers: Hawkestone cares less about that than hunting.'

'Well, I can do that without living entirely at the Castle. You'd soon get tired of me, Helen.'

'I hope, Harold, you've never had reason to think so.'

'Never. But make Hawkestone marry, and bring his wife to the Castle, and then your father will not want me to take his place. And then I'll come and be your guest as usual, for as long and as often as you like.'

'Perhaps Lord Falconberg can persuade you; I can't.'

At that moment, at a little distance in front of them, they came upon Lord Hawkestone.

For the first time in his life Harold Falcon imagined that he saw a difference in his cousin. It might be fancy, but he thought those broad, flat shoulders were somewhat narrowed and bent, and that the light active step was wanting in that firm but elastic tread, which he had so often admired as the Guardsman walked down St James's-street to go on guard or to attend a drawing-room or a levée. Was it only a listlessness which an idle country life is apt to engender, and which had been put on when he laid aside his bearskin, and returned to his home, to cheer his father, and participate in his sports, which he had done as soon as he could, after the terrible catastrophe which bereft the house of three loved children at once—leaving himself and Lady Helen to supply the affectionate care and honest gaiety, to which Lord Falconberg had been accustomed from his younger children? or was it really his own want of consideration for other people had blinded him to the fact that Hawkestone's health was not what it had been, and that the change of life from the jovial society of his regiment, and a town life, had truly wrought the indifference which he fancied he perceived in his cousin's gait, as he moved slowly up the hill before them?

I don't know whether my readers have ever noticed, as I have done, the extraordinary expression which is given to momentary character, impulse, or feeling, by the turn of a shoulder, or the limbs. Not of course to the extent of the countenance in depicting permanent sentiment; but so very strongly in those cursory movements of the mind with which a man may be affected by temporary anxiety, pleasure, fear, determination, or ill-health. If not, let me recommend to them a study of a well-known picture, the original of which is to be seen in the Duke d'Aumale's house at Twickenham. *Le duel après le bal* has exactly this point most strongly illustrated in the back of the successful duellist, a North American Indian, who is being urged from the ground by his second, dressed as a harlequin, while his victim lies in the very grasp of death, surrounded by his friends. The involuntary struggle to look back, if not to stay, or return to ask forgiveness and to close the eyes which are manifestly losing all consciousness of surrounding objects, notwithstanding the necessity for immediate flight, is manifested with marvellous power by M. Gérôme, the painter of a picture, one of the most powerful creations of the day.

Now it was just this idea that was presenting

itself to Harold when he saw nothing but his cousin's figure, as he passed from their sight round the last zig-zag that led to the terrace : he saw nothing of the face, no paleness, no weariness, no dejection, but that strange, unmistakable drag of the limbs, which, when not the effect of prolonged bodily exertion, is an invariable accompaniment of impaired health.

Harold's first impulse was to point it out to Lady Helen. His second to watch his cousin for the next week or two, and see whether there seemed to be any reason for his fears—fears which he knew he should rather allay than excite, unless some real mischief existed, which ought to be repelled. Helen was the last person in the world that he would like to pain ; and he knew well how quietly but how sincerely she would feel for herself and her father, should such suspicions, founded or unfounded, be excited. Harold Falcon knew little of her thoughts at that moment, or he would scarcely have waited till they reached the terrace to express them.

When they arrived at the second terrace, which was still another flight of long steps from the plateau on which the Castle stood, they found Hawkestone standing at the western angle, looking over the beautiful scene of wood and water, and so unobservant of everything else, that they came upon him almost unperceived. It was impossible not to notice the soft melancholy which pervaded his fine face as he looked over the vale and watched the sun going down behind the woodlands, now clothed in all the beauty of their autumnal dress. It was equally impossible not to see the forced smile with which he greeted them, and made a remark upon the exquisite scenery which had evidently affected him so painfully.

Lady Helen grasped her cousin's arm, and looked intelligently at him, while she spoke cheerfully enough.

'I thought you were out shooting, Hawkestone, with the duke and Mr Millbank.'

'No; I changed my mind. I sent Cartridge with them to show them the best beat; but I had a little headache. By-the-way, Harold, you might have gone, only the duke doesn't like shooting with more than two besides himself, and I really meant going.'

'Quite right too—that's one too many. I'll be hanged if I think we shall ever have such fun again as you and I used to have with Cartridge, in the holidays, when we came home from Eton. My poor father always said you spoilt me for any

good I should do afterwards, unless I meant to—'
and here Harold pulled up suddenly as if the recollection of his father's opinion was not calculated to give universal satisfaction to his cousins.
They saw his embarrassment and held their
tongues.

'Done anything, Harold, besides catching
these trout which I see in Helen's basket? There
are some good ones among them, nearly a pound
weight I should think;' and he looked into the
fishing basket which Lady Helen had just taken
up by the strap.

'Yes; I went out schooling on the new horse
for my uncle. He'll make a magnificent hunter
by the end of the cubbing season, if you think
he'll be quiet enough for him. If not, you'd better take him yourself;' but instead of replying as
he once would have done, he smiled good-humouredly but faintly, and turned round towards
the house.

'We'd better walk on,' said Lady Helen, 'it
begins to be chilly, and not very far from dinner-
time; the dressing-bell will ring by the time we
reach the Castle.' And here Lady Helen walked
off at a brisk pace, followed by Lord Hawkestone
and Harold.

Her ladyship reached the plateau on which

the house stood considerably in advance of the two gentlemen. They seemed in no great hurry; which, when we take into consideration the relative difference in time destined to *toilette*, between ladies and gentlemen, may not be surprising. Yet it could scarcely be so, for she lingered at the door by which they were about to enter.

Lord Hawkestone went off to one of the windows, by which he entered; Harold joined his cousin.

'Now, Harold, tell me do you notice anything in Hawkestone, or is it fancy on my part?' Harold had noticed already that he was lacking in tone, vigour, elasticity—in fact that five or six years had done the work of many, and just now he had fancied something more. Harold did not think so much of the difficulty of breathing which he had observed, as of Hawkestone's anxiety to conceal it.

'Country life, and absence of excitement. He doesn't look quite so strong as usual; but I see nothing to be alarmed at.'

'But don't you see that he cares so little about his usual occupations? he scarcely ever shoots, and exercise seems altogether distasteful to him.'

'Does my uncle think as you do, Helen?'

'I hardly know, but of course he would be

less quick to notice it than I. And Hawkestone dislikes so much any allusion to his health.'

'Then don't tease him about it, Helen, and I'll take an opportunity of observing him more closely.'

'And what am I to tell papa?' said she as she stopped on the landing-place before she turned off to go to her own room.

'That I'm not going yet for some time; and that—well, I'll stay as long as I can be of use to him;' and he turned off the other way. There was just daylight left for them to dress for dinner.

The party was large, but not brilliant. The Duke of Poictiers, an honest, sensible, popular man; a first-rate sportsman, a great judge of a horse, and—rarer still—of a hound; charitable, honourable, and a good husband and father—which are not great virtues for a man with a hundred thousand a-year, a charming wife, and a very handsome family; but not a wit. The duchess, middle-aged, very handsome, irreproachable in temper, character, and toilette. Lady Diana Belleville, their eldest daughter, in whose beautiful face that mixture of Saxon and Norman blood produced the best traits of both, large gray eyes, dark lashes and brows, standing out against the clear transparent skin and blue veins, with her straight well-formed features, and beautifully-shaped head. There were fine old country baronets and gentlemen, who supported the ducal interest on all occasions, talked poor-laws, turnpike-trusts, and turnips. As these subjects were uninteresting to Hawkestone's old friends and brother-officers, they made play with the baronets' and country-gentlemen's daughters, who were curious on the matter of the county-ball, the race-meeting, and the *on dits* to which the last season had given rise.

They were a good average set, in a large country-house, and all felt happy that Bitters was left behind somewhere. They could well forego the wit which made at least one person at table un-comfortable. They did not miss the astounding intellect of Highlow, who was quite regardless of the time or place in which he fired off his politi-cal epigrams, or the repartee of Barker, who, if he was not able to quarrel with somebody, managed invariably to set two others by the ears. There was no astonishing lion to monopolize the con-versation ; and if the duke was listened to with deference, it was certainly not because he roared louder than the rest of the company.

When Harold Falcon went to his room that night some serious considerations befell him, and

amongst all of them his cousin Lord Hawkestone
stood prominently forward. Was he as ill as
Lady Helen evidently thought him? He hoped
not, he thought not, but he would ascertain. And
Lady Helen herself? was it possible to know her
as he did and live with her, sharing all her anxieties and cares for those they mutually loved,
and not to love her? Was there anything so calculated to strengthen a bond which he rather
desired to weaken; which he sought to break—
and why? And when he came to this point in his
considerations, he was staring vacantly into the
once clear bright fire which had become necessary
with the chill autumn nights, but which was dying out rapidly now. Ah, that why? was his
secret; would there come a day when it could be
revealed?

Of himself it was impossible not to think in
connection with these subjects. How well he
remembered the time when the possession of such
a title and property would have saved him from
apparent ruin, and might have been welcomed
even at the sacrifice of such a cousin as Hawkestone. Yet, scarcely that; and now that he knew
him so well, and how dear he was to his uncle
and Helen, how gladly would he forego the possibility of such advantages to save them from a

moment's pain. How changed, how modified must all his feelings be !

And so they were. The truth was, that if Hawkestone Castle ever had been a prize worth sighing for, it had ceased to be so now. Harold cared nothing at all about it. Circumstances had happened in his short life which made him indifferent to the considerations which urge most men, and should to some extent move all. His wishes seemed now to be bounded by very moderate wealth—wishes which had once sacrificed an honourable position, and the esteem of others, as well as of himself, to their attainment—wishes which had given him sleepless nights and harassing days, and had ended in disgrace and ruin, but for an escape on which he dreaded to dwell.

Should he stay at the Castle if his cousin's health was deranged ? Could he help his uncle by doing so, without compromising himself or Lady Helen ? Harold was not a vain person, and he scarcely could come to a conclusion that his cousin would fall in love with him, without—well, modest reserve forbids the conclusion of that sentence, and his case was past praying for. He felt a wound, not ' as deep as a well, nor as wide as a church-door,' but it would do. He did love Lady Helen. Would to God he could tell her so.

CHAPTER XX.

A COUNTRY-HOUSE IN SEASON.

AND Lady Helen herself, how did she feel it? Well, that evening not at all. Harold had taken himself off from the billiard-room, or the smoking-room, under the plea of getting up at six a.m. on the following morning to go out cub-hunting. Lady Helen having no hounds to look after, nor any valid excuse for early rising, excepting virtue and health, was caught by the duchess and Lady Di, and Fanny Millbank, and Miss Montressor, to arrange the details of an excursion to see a robber's cave at some distance from them. The cave was only eighty feet from the ground on the flat surface of red sandstone, and the robber was said to have jumped in or out, I don't know which; but there were the marks on the red sandstone where his horse had alighted. The duchess went early, as pattern duchesses should do, to her own room, not certainly to see the duke, who was playing whist in the smoking-room ; but she left all the rest, who continued to tease Lady Helen about the horse they should ride, or which of the men should be told off to drive them, whenever the day of excursion should come. As Lady Helen said afterwards, from the length of time it took to settle, it might have been Wordsworth's Excursion itself. At last all went but Lady Diana, that handsome girl, with her half-Norman, half-Saxon face; and she would stop behind.

To say that Lady Diana Belleville was in love with Lord Hawkestone was to say what was not true. Still the gossips would say so.

'Well, and when's the young lord a-going to fetch his bride home, my lady?' said old Mrs Twoshoes, a privileged pensioner of Lady Helen's.

'Where should he fetch her from, Mrs Twoshoes?' inquires Lady Helen.

'Ay: but you'll know better than us old souls. Isn't it Lady Diana? Betty Gray tells me she's up at the Castle now.'

'That's rather as if she were coming to fetch him, granny,' replies Lady Helen, laughing at the conceit, which might have a little more truth in it than the other.

'Look, Mary, look, there's the duchess of

Poictiers, and Lady Diana Belleville, and there's
Lord Hawkestone with his back to the horses,'
shouts Miss Giggle, the bookseller's daughter at
Silverford, a small town half-way between Hawkestone and the duke's residence, to her youngest
sister: and the two rush to the front, as the
carriage drives rapidly by to the delight of all the
young women in the town. 'Why don't he sit
beside her?' says Mary, one of 'Nature's simple
children.' 'I'm sure I should sit side beside him
if I'd got a sweetheart.'

'Lor! stupid, don't you know that the gentlemen always sit with their backs to the horses?'

'Well, then, why can't she sit with her back
to the horses too? I'm sure she can't care much
about him;' saying which Miss Mary retired to
her work once more.

The great world didn't talk quite so openly
about it, although London society sometimes
wondered when it was to be. The *Mole*, a newspaper supposed to be wonderfully informed by
some tout on the confines of society, had hinted at
such a thing; and to this day the editor doesn't
know how very narrowly he had escaped a horse-
whipping. But there was, it must be admitted, a
tacit understanding among the Ladies Harriet
and Jane, and the Misses Montressor and the

Fanny Millbanks of the world, comprising scarcely the ten thousand that the *littérateurs* are so fond of talking about, that when Lady Di did not fall to Lord Hawkestone's share by right, she generally found herself in his neighbourhood by tacit permission of the rest.

The families too were very intimate. Separated by only fourteen miles of pretty good road, of the same rank and wealth, enjoying the same pursuits, and with families growing up or grown up, it was the most natural thing in the world that their visits should be frequent. The duke loved hunting, better even than racing, and had taken the hounds in a wonderful dilemma in the —— country, where all the great men in England hunted, and had forgotten to pay for even the covers, so absorbed were they in the main business for which they all came to ——. It must not be supposed that it was for lack of money, for as soon as the duke had relieved them of their fears, and the previous manager of his responsibilities, they came down in greater force and form than usual. He only gave it up and came back to Silverthorn—such was the name of his place ; where they cursed his hounds because they (the hounds) wanted to hunt, and his huntsman because he wanted to let them, and His Grace

because he wouldn't go forward to a hallo two
miles off before he had killed the fox he had
brought ten miles with him to what they called
that d—d forest. Being a fashionable country it
was soon taken by a racing banker, who had just
retired with a good fortune and plenty of ready-
money; and who, not finding the turf a letter of
introduction to the ladies of the *haute volée*, determined upon trying the national sport, irrespective
of expense, trouble, or abuse. In the language
of a well-known turfite at Newmarket, Mr Flash
having failed with Warren was going to try
Hunt.

Since that time the Duke of Poictiers had
passed his winter chiefly at his own place, and was
a constant attendant on the Hawkestone pack.
One of their best meets was on the duke's property, and the hounds were never at Silverthorn
without a large party in the house to meet Lord
Falconberg and his family. They shot together
in the season on their return from Scotland, and
when the covers of either were to be beaten, they
were always to be found among the guests at the
house of either. Above all things, they were both
of them what they called old-fashioned Whigs;
a bond of union which always seems to smell
of Charles Fox, but without one of the cha-

racteristics of that erratic statesman, but his *bon-hommie* and his good taste for a dinner.

The party, of which the duke and duchess had formed a part, had gone to fresh pastures. Others had come in their place. There had been more partridge-shooting, more fishing, and a day or two's cub-hunting, which had quite repaid even Captain Prestowe for the trouble of turning out a little earlier than at Melton. Harold was still there; and though he had kept watch and ward, with the hope of disabusing Helen's mind of her preconceived notions, and of comforting the old peer, who, it was evident, shared them, he had as yet detected nothing in Lord Hawkestone, nothing more than a little delicacy, which might be the effect of changed habits or ordinary causes. The season had not stood still, and though the sun shone brightly into Harold's windows, the beginning of October was at hand.

'Hawkestone,' said Harold Falcon, bursting into his cousin's room on the morning in question about eight o'clock, 'are you coming over to the pheasant covers. The hounds are to be there at nine this morning, and I heard my uncle go down ten minutes ago; he knocked at my door.' Hawkestone was still in bed, but awake, and answered, 'What's o'clock, Harold,'. at the same time ringing his bell. 'Eight! I felt so tired I thought it could scarcely be time to get up yet. Pull the blinds up, that's a good fellow.'

'Do you sleep with your window open? Your room feels cold.'

'Cold! No; I don't know that the window's open; and I don't feel cold. On the contrary, I perspire so much at night that I wish there was no fire in the room.' And Lord Hawkestone's valet came in and began to prepare his room. Harold Falcon went out, saying,

'We'll keep the breakfast, as Helen's going to ride, and won't be down till the last moment, I daresay.'

A handsome bridge ran from the one side of the park to the other, where the hounds were to meet; so that the distance from the house to the covers they were going to draw was scarcely a mile. There was no necessity for hurrying. The meet was likely to be a family party, as they did not profess to begin till the first of November in the open. Half-a-dozen farmers, who wanted to school their horses, might join them, in fact were sure to do so; as many county gentlemen in shooting jackets (their sons were once more at Eton and Harrow) would come out to have a look at the master and his young entries, and to get

some condition into the old horse, or to try the
new one.   There would be no scarlet, except in
the servants ; and the whole affair would be one
of business—to teach hounds and rattle the foxes,
with the chance of a run, if it happened to fall in
their way.

' Ah, Helen, this is charming,' said Lord
Falconberg, coming in to find his daughter
already drest and at the top of the table, with
Harold and half-a-dozen men making the most
of their time.

' Miss Linton and Lady Fanny, the pony-car-
riage is ordered for you, as you intend riding to
Silverford in the afternoon.'

' Why were we not allowed to ride with Helen,
Mr Falcon ? ' demanded one of the young ladies.

' Because your brother assures me that your
mare always runs away with hounds : and as he's
not here—'

' That's really too bad of Frank,' said Lady
Fanny Carysfort : ' he was short of horses last
year himself, and I lent her to him to finish the
season ; and his hands are so bad that she is inclined to rush at her fences.   As to pulling, a
child might ride her.'

'I've no doubt of it,' said Colonel Snaffles
tauntingly : ' and as we shall be out again only

five miles off at the end of the week, you shall ride her in spite of Carysfort, who is, as you say, a very bad horseman.' Here there was a little good-humoured laughter, as Lady Fanny was not disposed to allow any one to abuse her brother but herself.

'I don't say that, Colonel Snaffles : I only say it takes two to make a puller, and Frank's hands are not quite so good as—well, whose shall I say— ? ' Harold looked up at the *piquante* pretty little lady, who continued, ' Oh, I wasn't going to say yours, Mr Falcon ; though I daresay you think that's bad judgment on my part ; I meant to say Lord Hawkestone's.'

' Then here he is to acknowledge the compliment,' as the door opened and he entered the breakfast-room.

Lord Hawkestone looked, as all well-made, gentlemanly-looking men do, better in leathers and tops than in any other dress. Not that I for my part underrate the value of a straight well-cut pair of trowsers, Hammond's or Story's ; far from it. But from head to foot, a well-dressed horseman, who knows how to put on his clothes (for that's a very essential part of the business), is a sight better worth looking at than the best lounger that ever woke the flags of Bond-street or St James's with his Hoby's. If he has a leg that will hang from a saddle like the late James Mason, or the huntsman of Her Majesty's buckhounds, with the knack of making his boots meet his breeches in the same way, I should advise his following the example of Lord Falconberg, and wearing nothing else, until evening compels him to change them. It is difficult to get up a morning leg and an evening leg, for they are as different as the late Lord Petersham's snuffs; but if I must choose between the two, I take my stand on the morning leg. Calves, be it spoken with reverence, are vulgar.

Mr K—y, one of our best comic actors, was the occupant of a foreign railway carriage with a lady and her son. He slept well and soundly to all appearance the greater part of the journey. On some unexpected stoppage, the young gentleman, anxious to improve all opportunities of observation, remarked aloud—loud enough indeed to disturb the sleeper—'Ma, they're putting on calves behind.'

'There are a great many people,' said Mr K—y, with great gravity, 'who would be glad to do the same;' and went to sleep again. I am not one of those.

'Now, ladies,' said Harold, 'shall I ring the

bell for your carriage? You know the road, Miss
Linton, after you get over the bridge? The
hounds meet at the lower side of the cover, and
we shall draw up wind. And Lady Fanny, I'm
sure you'll not be angry if I remind you that
foxes have very quick ears, and don't like conversation.'

In a few minutes more they were all gone.

Nothing could be more beautiful than the
morning.

'Too gaudy for scent, I'm thinking, my
lord,' said Farmer Harrowgate, touching his
hat to Lord Falconberg, 'and a little east in the
wind; but there's been plenty o' rain lately, so
that it ain't very dry. Don't see none o' them
nasty cobwebs about neither.'

'I don't dislike a touch of east, Harrowgate;
you'll be glad to see Fearless again, he's grown
into a very handsome hound, and the best of that
litter: they're all very good too. Lord Hawkestone
likes them much.'

'Ah, my lord seems to take kindly to it. I
never thought he'd like the trouble so much as
you did. Always rode tremenjous too—him and
Mr Harold, ever since they was boys.

Then to each of his old tenants, as they came
up, Lord Falconberg had a kind word or two to

say; and though the old peer had aged wonderfully in the last four or five years, in fact since
the death of his children, still on horseback the
change was less perceptible than elsewhere. His
thin limbs clad in thick and loose buckskins,
beautifully made and cleaned; his straight, well-
cut top-boots, and the loose, strong black coat,
with its broad skirts and outside pockets, rather
concealed the stoop which was growing upon
him; and his handsome aristocratic face and gray
hair, almost white indeed, looked fresh-coloured
and bright in the morning air. His beautiful seat
showed well on a fine short-legged but thorough-
bred horse, whose head was so placed that the old
sportsman appeared to be playing with him, so
craftily was he restrained by the light but firm
hand that kept giving and taking as he pulled
first on one side of his bit and then on the other.

Lady Helen, too, must not be overlooked in
the crowd that began to assemble in greater
numbers than they had expected. Beautifully
dressed, beautifully mounted; she, too, had a
kind word for her father's friends, and managed
to remember the names of their wives and daughters as easily as she did her old pensioners in the
neighbouring village.

'How does the horse carry you, Helen—

nearly a handful isn't he?' said her cousin, as he
rode by her side—a gratification he never seemed
willing to deny himself. He was nearly a handful as she admitted; 'but not too much, as she
didn't mean to ride the run if they had one.'

'You shall have another bridle on that horse
another time. Your father quite agrees with me,
that you should ride him in a gag and a martingal, putting the martingal on the curb-rein.'

'It was Mr Curbs who thought it so dangerous; we spoke about it, at least Hawkestone did,
the other day.'

'He's like all grooms: if they've never seen
a thing, it can't be right. That's a good young
horse of Hawkestone's, Helen. I've been schooling him, and I persuaded him to ride him to-
day. I should like a run, though the country is
so blind. He'd soon find him out. He looks
better to-day.'

'But he's so indifferent about the whole thing,
Harold. Look at my father, he's more life in
him than Hawkestone now. Ah, here's the carriage.'

'What's the matter, Lady Fanny?' said Lord
Hawkestone.

'The ponies pull much worse than the mare,
and it's too bad of Frank, who only wants to

have her himself by persuading papa that I can't ride her.'

In five minutes more the hounds were in cover, and while Lord Hawkestone jumped his new horse over the fence with his hounds, his cousin Harold took the low stile in the corner nearest the river.

'That's right, Harold, put them to me; if we find, we've nobody but the new boy out this morning, and we'll try and force one or two out on the Grassfold side—we may get a gallop now,' and Hawkestone didn't seem to lack energy now at all events. The greater part of the field, some thirty or forty horsemen, headed by Lord Falconberg and Lady Helen, held on their way down the principal rides or on the outside, but so far back as to give the fox a chance of getting away.

CHAPTER XXI.

AN EARLY DAY WITH THE CUBS.

Young foxhounds are troublesome things to deal with : riotous, vigorous, courageous, and ignorant. These are not meant for their names, by-the-way, which they well might be. It was a beautiful thing to see them dash here and there with an indifference to thorns and briars, while here and there stood one or more with ears erect, looking as if they were rather surprised at their friends, and then dashing off for a hundred yards or more, whenever they found an open spot for their gambols. ' War'hare ! ' cries the new boy, cracking his heavy thong ; while the old lord and Lady Helen proceeded cautiously, the former taking note of the performance of his beauties, and marking some for distinction, in the hope of seeing them, in two seasons more, the perfection of what a hound should be. The real master, too, was at work with his head, and Harold was recording anything of notice for the evening's cigar, or the after-dinner conversation.

The scene was of great beauty. The night's spray hung still upon the leaves, as the dew upon the grass, though the sun was getting higher, and beginning to steal, here and there, through the red and brown autumnal tints. The ground game was quickly on the move, and it required all Harold's and young Jim's vigilance to keep the young drafts from occasional riot. Every now and then, too, a young cock, roused from his shelter, would rise through the branches, and fly to the other end of the long cover, while his more astute companions ran stealthily through the grass into the ditches and hedgerows on either side.

'Tally-ho!' sings out the family doctor, about a hundred and fifty yards down the cover, where he had stationed himself well out of sight, by Lord Hawkestone's desire; prepared, as all doctors are, to ride as if his limbs belonged to his neighbours, and he was to have the setting of them. 'Tally-ho!' yells the doctor a second time, which was not responded to, as the wily fox held his course out of sight along a hedgerow as impervious to vision as in the height of summer.

Crash through the branches, however, came

Lord Hawkestone, bringing with him two or three couple of his hounds, who immediately opened as they ran along the side of the cover, while the rest came joining in the chorus, hurried along by the joint efforts of Harold Falcon and young Jim. ' Hold up, stupid,' says the former, as his young horse, violent among the bushes, and endeavouring to get through, nearly falls on his head over some prostrate timber ; ' get away to him, Galloper,' while Jim hustled down the ride to see which way he broke, if break he would. Lord Falconberg held up his whip, and kept the impatient spirits behind him in check. ' Steady, gentlemen, steady—we've only young ones out to-day ; let's do the hunting first, you'll have time enough for the riding a month or two later.' Then there was a dead silence. ' Ah, he's back—I told you so—he'll not be out of these covers under half-an-hour, possibly not in double the time.' And then they trotted down the ride, keeping the hounds in sight. ' Hold hard, it's all the way back ;' and in another moment the body of the hounds came racing through the brushwood down the river-side, while the field turned round, as eager to go the other way as they had just been to follow the reverse.

By the time Hawkestone and Harold and Jim

had half tired their horses, when there had been
at least four foxes on foot at different times, and
when the young hounds had begun to settle, long
after the crowd had become impatient, and when
they had begun to talk about going home to
dress for market, a Hallo! Away! was heard from
the very point at which Hawkestone had wished
him to break towards Grassfold. The field turned
along the first broad ride that presented itself.
Lord Falconberg led his daughter at a pace that
soon put a considerable distance between them
and the broad-brimmed, red-nosed old fellows
behind. The doctor was fighting his way through
a grove of nut trees in full leaf, and seemed hopelessly planted; while Harold, performing his
promise to the best of his ability, took one turn
to bring up a refractory couple and a half, and,
leaving the rest of the laggers to Jim and luck,
emerged over a very unpromising blackberry bush
in full bearing, with his nose scratched and his
cheek bleeding. 'So much for doing the new
boy's duty, and letting Ned have a holiday to go
to Silverford fair.'

There was no time for much consideration.
On getting himself clear of the leaves, and his
horse's hind legs of a hurdle which he had brought
with him out of the blackberry bushes, the first

thing that he saw was a hat, which he recognized, just disappearing over a stiff-bound fence, one field ahead of him. On the right were the twenty-five farmers, confined to a bridle-road, with Lady Helen at their head, Lord Falconberg himself having emerged from the crowd, and in the act of negotiating what looked like a gap, only because the rest of the fence was impracticable. The business is soon told, for it was soon over. Farmer Harrowgate's notions of scent were all wrong. The young hounds, led by a lady or two remarkable for pace, never spoke after being once on their fox, but ran for Grassfold as if tied to him. They had done their hunting in the Hawkestone covers; and though Harold with Linton, Millbank, and some of his friends, tried hard to catch them, they never decreased the distance between themselves and Lord Hawkestone by a hundred yards.

'Look at those hounds, Linton; straight for Grassfold. It must be an old one; the quickest thing I've ever seen. Wonderful entry, and how little tailing.'

'Never mind the hounds, Falcon; look at Hawkestone's chestnut!' And true enough, he was performing over a difficult country after a fashion that betokened a good man was on his back.

But Harold's eyes were on the pack; and while Linton and Millbank were looking at the chestnut, Harold was looking at the hounds. The leaders turned to the left, which gave him one chance more; and while his late companions rode for a gate on the high ground, Harold, jumping an awkward staken-bound fence, sunk the hill at a pace that none but a thorough-bred one could accomplish, as the fox was pulled down in the next hedge-row.

He and his cousin were off their horses in no time, and the obsequies might almost have been performed by the time the field had arrived. Harold looked at Lord Hawkestone; instead of the bright fresh colour which he had usually seen, he was surprised to remark a paleness so great that he could not help saying,

'Are you unwell, Hawkestone?'

'Not the least; a little faint,' replied he, turning away from Lord Falconberg, who was on the other side of him. At the same time he looked at Harold intelligently, and blowing his horn, trotted gently forward.

'Where to now, Hawkestone?' said the latter, following him up, and seeing that his colour was returning.

'We'll go back and try the other side of our

covers. They want well rattling between this
and November. Thanks for the schooling you've
given this horse, he's quite perfect. Yours looks
as if he'd been plating during the summer.'

'I've only two, my dear fellow, and I regard
condition as the great secret of work. I ride
them all the year round, and they're just as fit to
go now as in February, and all the better for
their summering. There's no summering equal
to gentle exercise.'

'And yet Harold doesn't object to galloping
with me,' said Lady Helen, laughing, as she rode
up, 'when the road is like iron.'

'Because I always take one of Hawkestone's
horses. I suppose you're going home now. We
shall not get another gallop to-day, and are going
to have an hour's turn at business in the big
woods.' Saying which Lord Hawkestone and
Harold trotted off with about half-a-dozen of
their stanchest adherents—among whom were not
Linton and Millbank—to find another fox in their
nursery.

Lord Falconberg hesitated a moment, and
then followed the hounds down to the big woods,
where they had an hour's hunting and a kill
among themselves—quite a family party, and a
very dangerous one to the foxes.

'Where's Linton?' said Lord Hawkestone—
passing along the hall with a flat candlestick—to
Harold, who was coming the other way.

'Playing billiards with Colonel Montressor.'
The Colonel was a proficient, having commanded
a regiment in India which was always engaged in
fighting, pig-sticking, or billiards; and equally
adept at all three.

'Then he's happy. He quite delights in losing
his money, and the Receiver-General never fails
to accommodate him. Where are Millbank and
Carruthers?'

'They're in the smoking-room with Tommy
Dashwood. I'm going to my room to fetch them
some of those large Trabucos.'

'Are they all gone out of the drawing-room?'
inquired Lord Hawkestone, after a pause. 'You're
not going into *écarté* with Carruthers and Millbank?'

'Not I,' said Harold. 'I lost ten pounds yesterday, and I find it quite enough for such an
amateur as I. I should think it was like taking
a header to a man who never washed.'

'Time has been, old fellow,' said the other.
'Come to my room and let's have a chat. Bring
a cigar or two up; Helen don't mind it, and nobody else knows anything about it.' Saying

which he walked up-stairs slowly, and Harold joined him in ten minutes' time.

'How well those hounds behaved to-day, Harold.'

Harold Falcon was rather thoughtful, but said 'Yes' very deliberately. ı

'Confound it, Harold, you don't seem to think so. You're not thinking of your nose, though it was rough work on that lower side.'

'Well, I really do think so. That draft from the Badminton kennel is excellent, and I like your system of breeding from big hounds. This is a strong country, and requires plenty of bone as well as courage.' Then Harold drew his chair up to his cousin's fire, and made himself comfortable. 'Lend me one of your smoking jackets; that's capital. I'm glad you like your new horse. You've a good stud to begin the season. It's just the stud I should like. Like our clothes, it would fit either of us.'

'I'm glad of it, Harold.'

'When you're in the thick of it, I shall bring one more from Tilbury's, and see how near I can get to you. I was a field off this morning watching you, when the hounds swung round to my left. But, tell me, you were not quite well?' and Harold looked straight at his cousin.

'Ah, Harold—you detected it. Don't say anything about it to Helen or my father. I made up my mind to trust you! so let's have it out now. Don't bring any horses down from Tilbury's. Come and ride mine.'

'But, my dear Hawkestone;' and leaning forward on the arms of the chair, Harold looked very earnestly at his cousin.

'Listen, Harold—keep my counsel—I must go abroad the end of October or in November. It may be nothing; and I shall probably return all right. I wish my father to be spared all uneasiness, and Helen too, as long as possible. I would take you with me, Harold, but we want you here. You won't leave the old man, Harold, nor Nelly, will you?' Hawkestone seldom called her Nelly; never, indeed, but upon rare occasions of affectionate exhibition. Harold could scarcely answer, so unexpected was the conversation—but he did say,

'No. I'll not leave them: but tell me more. Have you seen any one? ₁ What are your reasons for wishing to go?' And the contending emotions which assailed Harold Falcon at once were not even explicable to his own heart. Sorrow had the first place, however, and a sense of terrible embarrassment mounted the colour to his face.

'Now don't fidget about it, that's a good fellow, and I'll tell you all about it. I have seen some one, and I think it better to act on his advice.'

'Cardiac or Lobel?'

'Neither the one nor the other. Cardiac would never have told me, nor you, nor my father, nor Helen; but he would have told everybody else. Lobel would have told none of us. He's the man who thinks you may eat ices, but you should have the chill taken off. No. I wanted the truth, and I went to Bluster.'

'Who has made a large fortune by frightening people, and then pretending to cure them,' said Harold, smoking easily to all appearance, but with his heart beating with anxiety. 'What did he say?'

'He told me what I feel to be true: that one lung is much disorganized, which means diseased, I presume; and that my days are numbered.'

Harold rose from his seat, unable to speak, and took his cousin's hands in his own. Twice he tried, but could say nothing. Lord Hawkestone seemed but little affected as he told his story, and continued to smoke as calmly as if he had never heard the startling intelligence, or was

talking of some one else. 'There, sit down,'
continued he, with a cheerful smile, 'don't be
too much alarmed. He told me the worst : that
I might live years with care and good luck, but
that I might be summoned at a shorter notice.
Come, Harold, cheer up, my old friend,' and as
he spoke, Lord Hawkestone got up, and leaning
over the back of his chair, put his arms affectionately over Harold's shoulders, whose grief almost
burst forth in sobs. 'I shall live long enough
now to give you all some trouble ; but it's right
you should know your position—better for us all.
Stop here and take care of your uncle and cheer
Nelly : no one can do it better.' Here they both
stood up on the hearth. 'And I say, Harold, let
me ride, and shoot, and look well or ill, as I can.
You know my secret—war' babblers, as we say
in the kennel—and God bless you, old boy.'

If ever a man felt miserable at a possibility,
it was Harold Falcon at the possibility of becoming an earl.

CHAPTER XXII.

EARLY MORNING IN ST JAMES'S.

TIME never stands still; and it did so no more with the family of Falconberg than with other people. Well-born wealth gets a few privileges out of the world, but this is one of the exceptions to that general rule, and common people ought to make the most of it. Great men are as subject to pain of body and of mind as little people, though not of the same kind; but they are obliged to come into this world and go out of it quite independently of their own wills or ways. I had forgotten—not quite—wealth will assist in life-prolonging, though it has no effect on life-producing: dirt, squalor, and misery seeming to claim as its own the blessings of a numerous off-spring. If the water-rates, or the rest of his creditors, are his enemies, Giles the curate does look ashamed when he goes to speak with them in the gate, if he has more mouths than he has bread for; and though there is nothing in our

religion from which some consolation may not be
derived, if properly applied, the application of
that full quiver to Giles's case, has given him less
satisfaction than it ought to have done, when he
has considered the necessity of maintaining them.
I have no doubt that when Providence sends
mouths it sends loaves. But if I get all the
mouths and you get all the bread—where are
we ?

Now the fact is that time did not stand still
for the Falconbergs, but their wealth had done
something for them in the matter of that other
case which we mentioned. It had prolonged
Lord Hawkestone's life in spite of some very strong
opinions formed by the physicians, and a certain
amount of indifference to his own case exhibited
by the young noble himself. He had been abroad
every winter, but he never would go till later
than the orders given. He would go out hunting
and take his chance of getting wet; and he would
ride much harder and much farther than he ought
to do; until he brought on that cough with its
bad symptoms, and that faintness, which he was
particularly ordered to avoid. He liked to
have a day's cover-shooting, and to look up the
woodcocks for which their woods were notorious;
and which birds, as the parson of his parish (a

fine sportsman as well as a divine) informed him,
did not come till the lessons were in Daniel—in
other words, in November.

Now what was to be done with a man of this
sort?   The best that could be made of Lord
Hawkestone by his sister and his cousin Harold
was a moderate valetudinarian from April to November.

It was April now. Lord Falconberg was just
come to town with his people, which consisted
still of Harold and Lady Helen, and a host of
retainers.   He looks older, and has one source of
regret which affects him deeply ; as deeply as ex-
terior circumstances can well affect such a man.
Beside and beyond the delicate health of his eldest,
and now only son, neither Lady Helen nor Harold
will marry.   They have both told him so at odd
times ; much to his disgust.   His first wish was
that they should marry one another.   But he was
much too delicate to hint at such a thing ; and
feeling conscious of his desire upon the subject,
he had not pressed Harold as much as he otherwise might have done, to come and live with
them.   That gentleman, therefore, was a guest
when he pleased, and as often as he pleased,
which was at least nine months out of the twelve.
But he still kept that little place which had come

to him with his aunt's money, not very far from London.

When Lord Falconberg found that Harold did not propose to Helen, but that all their liking for each other was a cousinly or platonic regard, he wondered why neither of them would marry anybody else. Lady Helen was still as handsome as ever. Farina had proposed, and been refused. He was a marquis, with a fine fortune, as much as Lord Falconberg had himself; but he was a great fool, and Harold hated the sight of him; which seemed quite enough to set Helen against him. She told Harold all about it, the old man knew, and the two schemers were unanimous in discarding the match of the season. But it was not so with Lord Belleville. They all liked him, and Harold and he were as intimate as ever. And they all spoke highly of him; but Helen would have nothing to say to him, though at this moment she was closeted with Lady Diana in Grosvenor-square; and there were half-a-dozen more hopelessly rejected. Hawkestone only made his health an excuse, which might have been accepted in peace and with resignation by the old peer, if he could but have seen Harold inclined to settle down. 'And here he is, not old but getting on,' as he told the duke, who, being himself midway between Harold Falcon's age and that of his uncle, thought there was plenty of time.

'Yes, duke, there's plenty of time; if I was but sure of his marrying at all. Hawkestone's health is very precarious.' And here the good old peer dropped his voice, for he loved Hawkestone dearly, and he knew the duke had an inkling of some feeling of the kind on the part of Lady Diana. 'Hawkestone's life is very precarious; and if that —— fellow George Falcon was to get the property, I think I shouldn't rest in my grave.'

'And what has George done?' says the duke, giving his weight-carrying hunter a reminder with the spur that he wasn't so good a hack as he might be. 'I thought he was one of the steady-going sort, Falconberg. Took a good degree; and when I saw him last was as full of law as an egg's full of meat. He's not quite so lively as my friend Harold; but young stock throws back, and his heir might be very different from himself; more like his father or his uncle. I didn't even know that he was married.'

'Nor do I know it, but I suspect it; and I could have forgiven anything but a *mesalliance*. I have heard that he really is married to some foreign woman or other.' And very savage the earl looked at the reminiscence.

'The devil he is! What makes you think that?'

'That sort of general report, which is not worth much, but which one can't disregard. It came from the Temple, I fancy, and got to the ears of old Dryden, who is pretty clever at ferreting out a mystery.'

'And infernally quick at finding a mare's-nest.' And then the two jogged on to draw Buttercup Gorse for an afternoon fox, and remarked upon the failure of scent in a season so dry as the present. Of course Harold and Lord Hawkestone had heard of all this; and the former especially had listened to it, and his uncle's violent protests against it; but as George had not been to Hawkestone or Grosvenor-square for a long time, it was not likely to be cleared up by direct explanation, a difficult process at all times; especially so in the case before us. Harold at all events did not seem inclined to stir in the matter.

Bond-street was full in the morning considering the time of year, not very late in April. It was especially crowded opposite Long's Hotel, and there stood Harold Falcon, unable to cross for two large waggons, which leisurely proceeded towards Bruton-street, and a very neat drag which was pulled up against the curb-stone at

Long's. No man about town could fail to recognize the drag. It was drawn by four short-legged
coaching-looking horses, worth from sixty to
eighty pounds a-piece; two roans, a dark bay,
and a good nutmeg-gray. The harness was
strong, well made, with a sufficiency of brass about
it, and exceedingly well cleaned, and an early
spring-flower adorned each horse's head-piece on
the outside of the blinkers. The coach itself was
rather low, and combined strength with lightness
and appearance; notwithstanding which it was
what Sir St V— C— was pleased to call ' coaching
all over.' It was a dark brown, picked out with
red, not showing too much colour; and on the
panels and boot was a plain crest. When Harold
detected what had been wittily called the ' clerical
tile and the fighting bird '—but which was a bishop's mitre and a dove with an olive branch in his
mouth—he looked towards the door of the hotel.
Of course he saw his friend Carruthers flourish-
ing a whip, which he had just caught, to the
damage of one of Mr Jubber's wine-glasses (he
had just taken the house), and to the hindrance of
a respectable gentleman who was waiting to get
through the doorway.

Carruthers was not much altered, not more
altered than a man should be who is married and

has given up steeple-chasing, and taken to driving
for an employment.   Fatter of course, and redder;
and at this moment given to a loud shawl of cash-
mere wound loosely round his neck.

'Why, Harold, when did you come to town?'
said the ex-country gentleman, shaking him
warmly by the hand; and it must be admitted
that (money matters on one side) Harold had not
a warmer admirer.

'I came up this morning from Egmont to
Grosvenor-square; the Earl and Lady Helen
arrived last week.'

'And how's Hawkestone? Is he coming home
soon?'

'Much better, I believe; he talks of coming
back immediately.   He hates the continent. But
nobody knows how he really is; for he always
makes the best of himself—he's so anxious to get
home.   Where are you going?'

'Down to Pinner to look at some horses.
You'd better come too.   There's Belleville and
Childers and two or three men want to look at
some horses of Mason's.   You'd better come.'
Saying which he took hold of the reins and pre-
pared to mount.

'Not to-day, Dick; I want to go to the club
for some letters.'

'Nasty place to get away from, this,' said Dick, once more looking round for his passengers. I wonder when it'll occur to any of those wise-acres, the commissioners, that this part of Bond-street wants widening. Who the d—l is to drive a team through here at five o'clock in the afternoon in June?'

'If railroads prosper as they have done there'll soon be no drags to drive, nor gentlemen to drive them. I came up on the Slough line this morning, and we did a mile a minute. In a very short time the street will be quite wide enough for all the drags that will go through it. How are Lady Margaret and the children?'

'All right, thanks. They come to town next month.'

'And the Rover?'

'Fresh as paint. I sold him last week for five-and-twenty pounds.'

'Stingy beggar,' said Harold, pursuing his way towards St James's-street, but soliloquizing, 'stingy beggar, I'd have given him the money myself to have turned him out, for old acquaintance' sake.'

When Harold walked down St James's-street, his mind turned back to other days. How different was he, how little changed everything

around him.   The Guards' club-house was transplanted to Pall-mall; and Crockford's, where he
had lost so many hundreds, was closed.   The
legislature, of which we are so proud, had taken
some very decisive steps towards making Young
England less extravagant in its taste for gambling.
To be sure it has failed, and has only turned into
fresh channels the waters that once ran through
Crockford's, Liley's, and the numerous houses,
where, in defiance of public opinion, men played.
Since those days we have become virtuous.   The
open profession of a gamester is illegal; and anybody may ascertain that fact who will visit Hyde
Park, or the rooms at Newmarket, or Tattersall's, or
the race-meetings of England in general. The dirty
little boys without money may not breathe upon
the glasses, it is true; while the sweet little dears
who have plenty may walk up, and assist at the
show.   This was a change, and Harold saw but
one way of ruining himself now, where there had
been several.   He saw however Young Strutt
going down in his bearskin, and he thought of
himself when he first joined; and was highly delighted that he had got as well out of his troubles
as he had.   At the end of some ten years he was
still paying the interest or the principal of the
debts he had contracted; but they were being

paid, honourably, and they still left him an income to live upon: thanks to his old aunt. As he thought of this, his step grew lighter, and he stopped for a moment to look at the caricatures in Sams' window, which exhibited some of his own friends in a very flattering light.

As he turned round the corner into St James's-square, he was stopped by the lively members of the new club, 'the Flag.' To judge by appearances he must have been a great favourite.

'Harold, my boy, how are ye?' said Major McMahon; 'you're just in time for lunch,' with which he seized him by both hands, to a certain extent monopolizing those members. At the same time he was surrounded.

'The very man,' says Strait Hare to his friend Brownlock. 'Falcon, you'll go down to the Woolwich meeting to-morrow; you can go on the drag. Slime is going to ride.' Harold had partly released himself by this time.

'It would be more to the purpose to tell me who's going to drive;' and then he passed up the steps into the club, followed by an old acquaintance or two, who wanted to talk to him.

'Bring a biscuit and some sherry here. Have you any news, Falcon?'

'None whatever. They say that Carfax will

be returned for Dumbleton; and that it will cost him six thousand. The last man spent five, and was hardly used. He lost his seat for bribing.'

'Bribing!' and the speaker's face was illumined with virtuous indignation.

'Yes; not high enough. There are places, you know, where they settle beforehand who's to have it; I hear that Carfax has arranged to have Dumbleton at that money, if he will close the bargain at once. That's the last political *on dit*. But I hear nothing at Egmont.' He was talking to his old friend Barrington.

'Then why not give it up. Lord Falconberg hates it, I heard him say so.'

'I must live somewhere—at least I must have somewhere to live. Besides, Lord Falconberg and Lady Helen like to have a place to run down to out of town. You'd better come and see us there—before Hawkestone comes home, or there will be no bed-room for you.'

'What's become of Hawkestone? Is he better?'

'He says so; I should fancy he was. But he's so imprudent. Just now he's in Italy, coming over the Simplon I believe, or else to Lucerne by Altorf, I don't know which. We expect him this month. It's too soon.'

'Somerville,' said a smart-looking light cavalry man on the steps of the Flag, 'who was that
very handsome man who went into the club with
Barrington and McMahon just now ? Wonderfully
good-looking fellow.'

'Don't you know ? That was Falcon.'

'What ! Falcon who was in the Guards ? '

'Yes, that's the man.   Did you see Slime ?
When Falcon came to grief in the Guards they
say that a thousand would have saved him. Well,
Slime was rolling in bank-notes, and a very
feather-bed sort of look it gives him ; so Collingwood proposed to Slime to lend him the money
on an emergency.'   To be sure the thousand
would not have saved him, but Slime didn't
know that.

'Of course he wouldn't do it,' said the light-
cavalry man, who had had some experience of that
kind, though the light-cavalry are very good in
bearing one another's burdens.

'Not he—he allowed him to be arrested on
the steps of his own lodgings in Maddox-street.
Falcon didn't know of Collingwood's application.
He would not apply to Lord Falconberg nor to
Hawkestone, either of whom would have given
him ten times the money. I suppose he didn't
like to do so, and Hawkestone was out of town.

At that time you know he had four cousins alive and well between him and the title, now he has but one, and that a most precarious life. I should think Slime was good for five thousand to-day on Falcon's I. O. U.

'Yes, if he carried interest enough. Stingy beggar,' added the smart-looking cavalry officer. So there was more than one stingy beggar about on that morning in April.

When Harold had finished his sherry and biscuits, and recruited his ill-informed mind with the *on dits* of the day, of which he heard nothing at Egmont, as he had said, he asked for his letters and walked out of the Flag. While he had been there, Lady Helen had had a visit too in Grosvenor-square. Lady Diana Belleville had come early to see her friend, and finding Lord Falconberg gone to a meeting at the Premier's, to see whether a cabinet minister's official residence was not paved with good intentions equally with another rather notorious place, she stayed to lunch.

The interesting regard which was attributed to Mr Slime will not stand out in such prominence when we consider that the fault, though gross enough, is not so uncommon as may be supposed. Slime acted by his instincts of the rat, which deserts a fallen house, it has been said. His thousand would have been useless, had he offered it, we know; and it was far better that Harold should have borne his own burden, if he did not choose to give one end of it to his own family. There were plenty more besides Slime that knew of his difficulties, but none of them, that we heard of, came to the rescue. All we can say for Collingwood himself is that he was hard-up; so were some others, which Slime was not.

CHAPTER XXIII.

OUR RELIGIOUS EXERCISES.

SOME few years before the time of which I am
writing, and about seven-and-thirty years before
our own, there was a strong religious movement
in Oxford. I say in Oxford; for although it soon
began to pervade other parts of England,—as
what extravagance will not!—it was so much
more Oxonian in its locality and tone, as to be
even distinguished by one name, among many
others, as the Oxford movement. Eminently
prolific of good and evil, the former predominat-
ing.

Beyond this it was Puseyite, Newmaniacal,
Anglo-Catholic, High Church, and Ritualistic.
It was difficult to say what it was not, according
to the tenets or prejudices of its denominators.
Its earliest professors were remarkable for many
things not before understood in the University.
It met with favour from neither the old orthodox
divine of the Common Room—who liked its port

and its piquet, and who limited himself to a certain number of chapel attendances, lest he should by voluntary religious exercise be considered to savour of Popery ; a new feature in that obligating creed,—nor from the undergraduate, who, whatever penance he might imagine that he suffered by the Oxford *Curriculum*, had no idea of making a sacrifice of his personal self-indulgence part of his religious profession, any more than of his practice.

Its first professors, some of them, I say, were remarkable for shining ability, great logical acuteness, much learning, and deep thought. They were also endowed with perseverance and logical courage to carry out to its fullest extent their crotchets ; and having embarked on a special voyage, were not to be daunted by the dangers that beset them when they got amongst the breakers. Hence came a great loss to a good cause ; the loss of men to the Protestant Church, whose zeal and talents could ill be spared. There are always men to follow a lead, and those who had themselves gone thus astray, drew some weak followers after them. This was sure to be the case. For just as Charles Dickens may be regarded as the greatest enemy the English language has ever had, by the host of servile imi-

tators his excellence has procured for him, and
who have not been able to distinguish his faults
from his virtues ; so that smaller and less capable
herd of imitators have mistaken the weak points
of the original seceders for their excellence, and
have left the Church little to regret in their
secession, beyond the sorrow she feels for their
own misadventure.

The sacred spring, however, from which these
troubled waters flowed, was anything but dried
up ; and in process of time it has poured forth a
stream, which, with all its obstacles and impedi-
ments, and the natural impurities of the soil
through which it runs, is fertilizing and rendering
productive vast plains, which were before this but
scantily benefited by religious irrigation.   In
plain language, Puseyism, or Ritualism, or whatever you may choose to call that movement in
our Church which originated with Oxford some
two-and-thirty years ago, has given rise to an
amount of work and sentiment—call it excitement
if you will—which has been universally advantage-
ous.   Puseyism has done good, a great amount
of good.   It has taught men to think, and sent
men out to work ; it has revived in its integrity
the old Parochial system, it has brought to our
door (or taken us to theirs) the poor, the ignor-

aut, the unwise.   It has promulgated the best
charity, love for God through our fellow-creatures.
So we must not laugh at its absurdities, for it has
them; nor confound its unwise, and in many
cases insincere, advocates with those men and
women whose hearts are in their work, and who,
distinguishing the corn from the chaff, are willing
to let both grow to the harvest lest they should
root up the good with the bad.

'Hallo! look at Lenten,' says young Wild-
boys of Ch. Ch.; 'don't suppose he ever had
a bath in his life.'

'Nor a bottle of champagne,' adds Chaffinch,
of Merton, as that erudite and cadaverous, but
rather slovenly and unworldly, gentleman the
Reverend Benedict Lenten walks up the hall,
with his hands in front of him, a pious contrast
to his pious friend the Reverend Amos Kitten,
who affects the innocence of youth and the play-
fulness of girlhood, as a becoming mark of his
Anglo-Saxonism.

'Great expense of candles there, Goldstick,'
says the Honourable Rigby Passenham, who has
lately taken to going to church and is very observant.

'Yes,' says Lord Goldstick; 'but you wait a
bit, and you'll hear a magnificent "credo;" and if

we have that anthem of Montem Smith's you'll be delighted.'

'Who's that just come in?'

'That's Pulham, the man who had to leave the Flag for a turf robbery; and the good-looking man with him is young Spoonington, who ran away with old Covey's wife.'

'Well, he's none the worse for coming to church,' says the newly-converted Passenham, whose reflection kept pace with his observation. 'Look at those black women!'

'I don't see any black women,' says Goldstick.

'There; near the reading-desk, with curious head-dresses; look as if they were bald.' And true enough some curious specimens of Anglican conventualism were there.

'Those are the *Sœurs de Charité*,' says Goldstick again, who was getting tired.

'By Jove! but I say, old fellow, that's rather strong, isn't it? Belgian, or something Catholic?' Passenham was not yet up in the business.

'We're all Catholic, too,' replies Goldstick, whom long practice had made more *au fait* at the language, and who, indeed, had more sense than the other, and was rather amused at his friend's mystification. 'We're all Catholics.'

'Ah, yes; I see; so we are, to be sure, since the Reformation.'

'This is a new light, Mary, dear,' says a lady in the body of the church opposite the altar. 'What a beautiful altar-cloth; and do look at those vestments, why they're real jewels.'

'—sh, ma, dear!' Ma dear spoke a little above high-church pitch. 'That's the diamond that was given by Lady Sophia Crosspatch; it was sewn into the cross at the back of the chasuble.'

'What's a chasuble, Mary?'

'Well, I don't know exactly; but it's absolutely necessary, Mr Longfast says, to make the services complete.'

And that's the way the world goes on. But I know Goldstick would not come but for the music, nor Passenham but for Goldstick. Pulham is not bored by the service, and Spoonington is balancing accounts by his attendance. Mary's mamma is not altogether at her ease; but Mary herself sees an all-sufficient reason for self-denial, early rising, alms-giving, and a mild good-humour in the adornment of her favourite curate, Mr Longfast, in stoles, chasubles, albs, copes, and a flowery garment, with a cross of four feet long.

It ought to be remarked that a great many persons who allow their virtues to begin here do not limit them to these externals of propriety.

The position of the Church may account for the conversation which was taking place in Grosvenor-square, while Harold Falcon was lounging about Bond-street and the clubs.

Lady Helen sat in a handsome *prie-Dieu* in her own room, and opposite to her Lady Diana was reclining in a comfortable arm-chair. A little fire gave additional warmth to the room, well carpeted and curtained, and furnished with all the luxuries which well-disposed wealth could procure. There was an ormolu cabinet of very handsome workmanship; some beautiful specimens of old Sevres china, of which she was very fond; some cabinet pictures, gems which had been given to her by Lord Hawkestone; and there was an utter freedom from all the fopperie of upholstery which were then so common, and which were unfortunately taking an ecclesiastical turn. Altars, crucifixes, and statuettes of virgins, saints, or martyrs, were wanting; yet Lady Helen Falcon was a very good and a very religious woman.

'And do you go regularly, Helen, every Thursday to your district?' inquired Lady Diana, whose bonnet was lying on a chair near her, and whose beautiful fair hair was floating about, as it sometimes did in those days, without any suspicion of her being a bigamist, poisoner, or even a malicious slanderer.

'Always; unless something extraordinary occurs to prevent me.'

'And where do you dress, dear?'

'Where do I dress?' repeated Lady Helen, not quite understanding the question; 'what do you mean, Di?'

'I mean,' said the laughing lady, 'where do you put on your black serge dress, which all you Sisters of Charity wear when you go visiting?'

'But I don't wear black serge, my dear,' replied the other.

'Oh, I don't think its anything without the dress, Helen. I shouldn't feel half charitable—no, I don't mean that—I mean half up to the work.'

'Perhaps not; I daresay some ladies do not: and then Mr Carfax (he was the brother of the Member for the corrupt borough of Dumbleton) encourages them to enter the order. It never occurs to me that I should do more good in one colour than another.'

'But it's so becoming, Helen, dear.'

'Not to dark people like me, Di,' said Lady Helen, laughing, 'though it might suit you.'

'And who are the other Sisters?'

'But I'm not a Sister. Of course, as you will understand, all the Sisters are light-haired blonde beauties.'

'Well, the other ladies who assist in the district visiting?'

'Some are friends of our own—the Carletons, Mrs Melville, Dora Shakerley, Lady Margaret, and half-a-dozen more.'

'You must have quite a jollification. And are they all of that class?'

'Not entirely; there's Mrs Panns, the ironmonger, and—'

'That must be rather a bore, dear. Does she dress in serge?'

'Not at all a bore, dear,' said Lady Helen, answering the first part of her friend's speech. 'She doesn't dress in serge, and she often goes with me. She's a very good woman, and does a great deal of good. I think I prefer Mrs Panns to any of them. I found out her trade by her getting a quantity of kitchen utensils for the poor old women at cost price. She made no secret of her business, for she told us all that her husband would provide them for next to nothing.'

'And do you think Mr Carfax would take me? I should so like to do some good, Helen; one would go into society with such an easy conscience.'

'I don't think he'd care about the compromise, dear; but as we must go into society, and live like other people, it's as well to have regular times for doing other duties. One can't be always out of the world, and one ought not to be always in it.'

'Then I'll go to Mr Carfax to-morrow, if mamma will let me; and I shall ask for permission to enter the order.'

'And if you find it becoming, let us see you in your dress, Di. We expect Hawkestone home in a short time, and he'll be glad to see you.'

'He will?' said the girl, unconsciously betraying her interest in Lord Hawkestone's opinion by getting up and kissing Lady Helen.

'There's nothing he likes so much as self-denial, or self-sacrifice of any kind, in woman, Di; but I think he'd prefer it without the serge.' And there is no knowing how far the confidences might have extended had not the door opened, and Harold Falcon been announced.

Harold Falcon put a stop to an interesting conversation, which exhibited the sentiments of two ladies, identical in result, but somewhat different in principle. He was always a welcome guest at his uncle's, as the reader knows, and no less to Lady Helen than to the rest of the circle. He looked at present out of sorts, rather than spirits. These latter were never very high. In that respect he had changed very much. The devil-may-care ease of a *mauvais sujet* much in debt had given place to the sobriety of a well-to-do man of the world. Whether these highly-bred rascals, who go about with their hands in other people's pockets, laugh at their own success as compared with the losses of their creditors, it is hard to say. A great many of them sleep very well, and are not surprised at it. They are rather surprised that sleep should visit the temples of those to whom they owe so much, without the prospect of paying it.

' Helen,' and Harold Falcon had no scruples about making Lady Diana Belleville a confidante, hoping some assistance from her, ' here's a letter I found at the club, from Hawkestone ; he's on his way home—he does not say whether better or worse; but he's going, as usual, to do the stupidest thing possible.'

' And what must I do ? '

' Stop him. Write at once.' A close observer would have seen colour and disappointment blend in Lady Di's cheek as he said so.

'Stop him? That's not so easy; but is he worse?' and Helen's voice betrayed her anxiety.

'No, not at all, that I know of; but he will attend to you. Stop him from going home by Holland. I know the country—cold and bleak at this season; let him come as usual, straight by Paris. There's a railroad now from Strasburg, and he will travel with less fatigue.'

'But if he will come through Holland, who's to prevent him, Harold? Which way does he want to come?'

'He speaks of Luxemburg and Cleves. I know the country well. He wants to see Nimeguen and some of the Dutch cities. Persuade him to come straight home.' And Harold Falcon seemed to attach much importance to it.

'But he's not so easy of persuasion, you know.' Still Harold urged her. He seemed much bent on his cousin's avoiding Holland; and, of course, after a few more words, Helen gave way. Lady Diana seconded Harold's remonstrance; and so feebly that it was clear enough she had some reason for ardently desiring to succeed.

'I'll write by to-night's post, Harold. I shall

be so glad when he is home again. When are we to go down to Egmont?'

'You'll be my guests, Helen, at Easter. I've been down to put everything to rights for your reception. I've no room for you, Lady Di, or we should be delighted to see you—at least Helen would do the honours for me.'

'Certainly, with the greatest pleasure, Di. But it's a terribly stupid place, according to Harold's account. This is our first visit.'

'We can send the horses down, and ride about the country. We've a new squire, too, who's worth seeing—Sir Samuel Cripplegate— otherwise there's literally nothing for ladies to do in a suburb.'

Croquet hadn't yet been invented.

CHAPTER XXIV.

THE JANSENS.   MOTHER AND SON.

TIME had also gone on with Bernhard Jansen
and his daughter, and had changed to eternity
with his wife.   Frau Jansen had been dead some
few years.   No clock had stopped, no mysterious
symbol had betokened the inopportune death of
our old acquaintance.   She was missed, when she
did go; as any one may be, without compliment
in saying so.   A dead wife may have been the
tree that sheltered the family roof from storms
or strokes, but she may too have represented the
thunder-cloud that towers above us to pour down
her vials of wrath, when the family atmosphere
had reached the proper temperature.

Jansen felt her loss, when she did go; which
is an euphemism upon my previous expression,
'missed her.'   So did Margaret.   She had been
kind to Margaret in her peculiar way; bent on
her marrying a gentleman; indulgent, alas! to
her faults; unconsciously her worst enemy.   But,

thank Heaven, children are not made to see in-
dulgence in that light, whatever its results.
Should you like to see a monster in human
shape? I'll show you one—a phantom, a myth,
I believe; as impossible, or more so, than Becky
Sharpe herself. It is the man or woman, of
whatever age or condition, who turns round upon
the authors of his or her existence, to cast in
their teeth the half-venial selfishness of child-in-
dulgence. I say nothing of faults, of other faults.
No man of common sense can shut his eyes to
facts; but few would reject the burden of his
own infirmities to put it on the shoulders of a
parent's over-love.

So Margaret missed her mother, indeed. Years
had softened old Jansen's nature, and made his
bark less loud as he had one less to bite, or as
he found a more ready submission to his will.
Most men cease to fight when there is no resist-
ance. The two lived on in the cottage near
Cleves; and the changes that had taken place
are easily told.

There was no Frau Jansen, I have already
said. In the next place, the man Jansen was no
longer a handicraftsman. He and his daughter
together had enough to live upon well, in a comparatively cheap country, so he worked now only

en amateur. He sometimes took a turn to great cities, to the picture-galleries, and the churches, and the curiosity-shops of his country; but he had ceased to work at his art, and money would not tempt him. He was getting old. The giant was still large, heavy, massive, but no longer quick of foot, nor upright. His hair was gray, and so were his shaggy eyebrows, and they over-hung his still quick, intelligent eyes. He was much altered since he left England, and per-haps, but for his great height and size, he would not have been recognized as the old ring-man and money-lender, excepting by his intimates—Harold Falcon certainly among the number.

It was a regular April day, though May was about commencing, when old Jansen and his daughter sat in a neat little room, furnished in a less primitive style than usual among persons of Jansen's class in that neighbourhood. Being half English himself, with a daughter entirely so, he had transplanted his notions of comfort to his own country, as far as he could; for Cleves is in Guelderland, and he was a Dutchman. There was a good easy-chair of real English build, some warm curtains, which darkened the little room; he still clung to the stove instead of a fire-place; and there was a gaily-patterned carpet, not tacked

down as in our houses, but let to lie loose on the
floor, which was polished, and bore to be denuded
of its covering, when summer was fairly set in.
For the rest, Herr Jansen was occupied drawing,
while Margaret was engaged on that never-failing
source of self-congratulative German industry, a
stocking.

'Margaret,' said the old man, 'where's the
boy ?'

'He's coming from Emmerich : I expect him
at Cleves this afternoon. He should be home
in an hour or two.'

'Do you feel satisfied with his English ? He
seems to me to speak it scarcely so fluently since
he left Düsseldorf.'

'He had great advantages there,' said the
lady to her father; 'he was always in the English
clergyman's house, excepting when studying at
the gallery, or with his masters. Since then it
may be that he speaks less easily.' Herr Jansen
and Margaret always conversed in English, excepting when occasion required—as before others,
their neighbours—that they should speak German.

'And what do you propose to do with him
now ?'

'I think of doing as you recommended. Let

him go to the English tutor at Heidelberg, and
when old enough send him to England.'

'Why not to the German university?' inquired her father. 'A university life is a great
thing. He will acquire a knowledge of the
world.'

'But it is a very different world from the
English world, in which I hope he will move.'

'You are bent on an English career for him?'

'I am. I have no other wish. You said you
thought it might be gratified.'

'I think so still. But have you still so strong
within you the same desire, the same hope, the
same expectation. To me it seems vain. We
have seen him no more, have heard of him no
more. Give me the boy. Let him turn to art.
It is still time. He has a fine perception: and
here, at least, it is an honourable occupation.'
Herr Jansen seemed very much in earnest; as
though he had a love for the boy of whom they
spoke, and as of one for whom he meant to do all
he could. Certainly Jansen's notions of true
greatness were centred in art, though he had
tried a shorter road to money once on a time.
But he was made up of mixed motives, not comprehensible to every one, nor always to himself.
Art, he said, was the highest sagacity, and money

the highest necessity. But art did not pay such high wages as the devil, and once he had changed his sides. Now that he did not want the wages, he should like to go back again. But how about the boy?'

'Papa,' said Margaret, looking steadily at her knitting, but letting her fingers cease their active employment, 'I owe you much, I wish I could pay you for the sorrow I have given you,'—and here a tear fell upon her work,—'but I can't. Take my boy; he is yours, if you will have him; but you know my hopes, and they can only be accomplished in my way.'

'There, no more, Margaret; I'll do my best for you. I'll go to England when I can, and see what is best to be done in the matter; till then be still, my good girl. We've both had our sorrows. It's best to share them.'

Then he assiduously applied himself to his drawing, and bent over it more closely than usual; and his daughter went on with her knitting.

'Don't you think it odd, now, that so many English travel, and so few come this way? Nobody ever goes to Cleves, excepting the Dutch, that we ever hear of.'

'It's not the direct road anywhere. But I

saw an Englishman yesterday at Herr Maivalt's at the *table d'hôtc*. He was going to Amsterdam by Nimeguen, I think he said.'

'What was he like?'

'A milord of course. However, he really was so. Lord Hawkestone, on his way from Italy. Why he should have preferred this road, I can't conceive. He was ill too ; at least he looked so.'

'Perhaps only tired. Lords do tire sometimes of pleasure—it's a privilege they enjoy in common with other people.'

'He might have gone by Strasburg. There's a railway to Paris. Perhaps if we get one, the beauties of the Clevischeberg might become known. There's no doubt that your countrymen— *yours* I mean, Margaret—might learn something from intercourse with foreign countries.'

'They've learnt nothing yet ; and there's little good they could learn.'

'So they think themselves. They've not been far enough, nor staid long enough, nor in sufficient quantities. Send them to France, with their stiff stand-up collars, and tall hats, their unsociable manners, and pride of purse, closely-shaven chins, and tightly-strapped trowsers—'

'To return with manners as loose as their neckcloths, slouched hats, pockets down to their knees, and an affectation of gaiety which is worse than our ill-humoured reserve.'

'It will be better for both, Margaret. Travelling will do them good.'

'It will be worse for us, papa. What pet virtue is France to carry away from England?' Jansen stopped and then said slowly, and bitterly,

'A taste for horse-racing, and that indomitable coolness in wickedness—no, no, let's shuffle the national vices. You'll see that, by the time this world is a great network of railways, the Englishman and the Frenchman will be both more agreeable companions, and—'

'Worse men.' Bernhard Jansen had risen before his daughter uttered these few words, and it was plain to see that his humour had changed. He ran his hand through his gray locks, which were long and silky. Then he clenched it sternly, turning away from his daughter who had taken possession of the other hand, and said with suppressed voice and emotion, 'worse—impossible. S——,' here he swore a terrible German oath; 'that you, too, Gretchen, should live to say it.' She let fall his hand and returned to her seat, cowed and dejected. The old man went out.

Margaret Jansen is, notwithstanding increased age, worth a few moments' consideration. She is as beautiful as when we first saw her, as the assistant glove-cutter in the Woodstock man-trap, so skilfully baited. There were the clear blue eyes, full, rather far apart, the white low forehead, the hair a light brown, perfect in quantity and quality, the lily reigned in her cheek, the rose was dead or had left only its scent, and the bright lips parted showed the pearly teeth, as of old. Of course she looked older—matronly —and the curls which formerly clustered round her temples, and descended to her neck, were now reduced, curbed from their luxuriance into simple bands. She was a very pretty woman.

Before I go on with the story, I must account for Bernhard Jansen's peculiarity of humour by recurring to the events of past years. It will be remembered that he has been described as a vio-lent, overbearing person, at times, but with a great amount of rough good-humour, and an easy willingness to act with generosity. Circum-stances acted upon this temperament at first very disadvantageously. His wife was unsuited to him in many respects, and had that narrowness of understanding which such men are of necessity apt to despise.

One of his characteristics, too, was a love for his daughter, which was warmer as it was less

demonstrative than is usual. It was thwarted
by the conduct and injudicious manœuvres of
Frau Jansen and of the daughter herself. With
an honesty of purpose which the giant carried
with him in his face and very *physique*, he had
denounced their wicked and silly designs for
achieving a position of very doubtful happiness
and possible disgrace.

From the day that they had reached their
present abode in the neighbourhood of Cleves,
the man's mind to some degree had given way.
All its consistency had broken down when he
heard the secret of his daughter's dishonour. It
had become necessary that he should know the
truth, that the honour of his name and family
had been stained in the person of his only child;
for within five or six months of their leaving
England, Margaret was a mother.

At first, violent paroxysms of rage were succeeded by long fits of silent sullenness; when
the dishonour was inevitable, by a settled gloom.
It was necessary that the best should be done for
the girl, and his violence would but endanger her
life, and increase the chance of detection. He
was silent that others might be so too. For a
twelvemonth he would see neither the one nor
the other; for he believed his wife to be the more

culpable of the two. Perhaps she was, but her daughter would not tell her so. She joined them on the continent in time to render every needful assistance, having remained in England to pack up their effects.

In a few years the mother died, of cold, or of heat, or of some of those inexplicable disorders of which men and women do die. From that time the old man grew calmer, but he grew older; and as he grew older he became exceedingly fitful in humour. The odd part of it was that he loved the boy with a fondness which he had once felt for his daughter. He wanted him to study art in Germany, his mother desired that he should go to England. Either would have given way, and from different motives.

A word for the boy himself. He was a very handsome young fellow, with laughing blue eyes, and curly hair, essentially Saxon in appearance, and very English in manner and figure. This Anglicanism had been confirmed and improved by constant association with English boys at his tutor's at Düsseldorf, where, with Latin and Greek, and other needful scholastic accomplishments, he had acquired a facility of speaking our language, which defied detection on the score of his supposed foreign origin. Till he was seven or eight years old he may be said to have rejoiced in no name at all. He was first called Baby, and then George, and it was not until after Mrs Jansen's death, and when it became necessary to part with him, that a name had to be sought for him. His mother had her way, and he became a fellow-pupil of several young English lads, as George Fellowes. Old Jansen submitted easily to what he could not quite comprehend. He ventured upon some suggestions, which were not heeded by Margaret, and in the end consoled himself with the reflection that, as long as it were not his own name, it would be well to let her have her fancy. 'She has suffered more than I, though she has deserved it.' He was also well content to love the boy, as much as he now professed to hate all Englishmen. 'Fellowes? why not, as well as another. Heaven knows whether the poor girl believes her own story or not.'

 END OF VOL. I.

JOHN CHILDS AND SON, PRINTERS.